THE DERBY MAN IN ACTION

"We're trapped, Darby. There's six of 'em and Claude Tulley all by hisself is enough for both of us."

But those odds couldn't stop the Derby Man, Darby Buckingham. He had a winning fighting formula that was brutally simple—you hit fast and you hit hard. No backward steps and absolutely no hesitation. Above all, even if you were badly overmatched and outnumbered, you never showed fear.

So, like a cannon shot, he hurled himself at the cruel giant, Claude Tulley. Take out the strongest and sometimes the others would lose their stomach for the fight.

In the moment before closing, he saw a flicker of alarm in the giant's face. Before he realized it, Darby's fist blurred through the air, sliced between Tulley's upraised guard, and exploded against the jawbone. One of Darby's knuckles cracked and pain jolted up his arm. But he ignored it. When Tulley's mouth flew open, Darby pounded an uppercut to the stomach and Tulley pitched over face first.

Then the other five closed in . . .

The Pony Express War

Gary McCarthy

BANTAM BOOKS · LONDON · TORONTO · NEW YORK

To Glendon David, my littlest cowboy

THE PONY EXPRESS WAR
A Bantam Book / August 1980

ISBN 0-553-14185-6

Published simultaneously in the United States and Canada

Bantam Books are published by Bantam Books, Inc. Its trade-
mark, consisting of the words "Bantam Books" and the por-
trayal of a bantam, is Registered in U.S. Patent and Trademark
Office and in other countries. Marca Registrada. Bantam
Books, Inc., 666 Fifth Avenue, New York, New York 10103.

PRINTED IN THE UNITED STATES OF AMERICA

0 9 8 7 6 5 4 3 2 1

The Pony Express War

Chapter 1

Darby Buckingham puffed rapidly on the Cuban cigar and his black mustache bristled as he read the letter aloud to the voluptuous Dolly Beavers.

February 20, 1860

Dear Darby:

As you are well aware, your latest dime-western novel about mustangs has been tremendously well received by the loyal army of Buckingham readers. The book is also enjoying immense sales on the European continent. Congratulations!

What are your future writing plans? Believe me, as your friend and publisher, I do not wish to hurry you nor alter the tried and true creative processes that have marked your already illustrious writing career. However, the staff editors of the New York Publishing House and myself are in agreement that you are in a most favorable position to chronicle one of the greatest enterprises in American history—THE PONY EXPRESS. This time, the mighty freighting company of Russell, Majors, and Waddell has, perhaps, put itself to an impossible task. THE PONY EXPRESS is to traverse this vast continent between Missouri and California—1,966 miles—in an unbelievable span of ten days. It is a visionary concept, probably conceived in the desperate hope of obtaining a government mail subsidy across the heretofore unconquerable Central Overland Route.

Most of the eastern financial society believe the enterprise to be a foolhardy gamble. But the public is aflame with excitement and the very mention of Pony Express stirs the blood. Please consider journeying to the western terminus of Sacramento and centering your next story

around this historic event. Such a book could be your
greatest yet.

> Sincerely,
> J. Franklin Warner
> President, N. Y. Pub. Co.

Finished and quite sure he had not misread a single
line, Darby tossed the letter to the floor of the John C.
Fremont suite and lapsed into an indignant silence. It
galled him deeply that Mr. Warner had the nerve to
suggest an assignment. It galled him even more that
he'd already decided to go to Sacramento and investigate the commencing of the Pony Express. Now, blast
it, J. Franklin would think it had been *his* idea. That
was bad: Darby had the feeling there would be other
"ideas" coming from New York until, eventually, he
would be no more than a highly paid literary lackey.

A fiercely independent man, Darby's senses were
finely tuned to any potential threat to his freedom; his
practice, therefore, was never to follow anyone's direction. So far, his instincts had guided him from those
early years in New York where he'd fought his way up
the ranks to become a bare-knuckles champion. Heady
times, those, but not particularly profitable. After a two
year reign, he'd beaten all comers but knew it could
not last. Besides, it seemed to him the crowds were becoming less interested in the sport and more interested
in seeing blood shed—anyone's.

"Kill him, Darby, kill him!" became a familiar cry at
his fights until, one night, Darby almost *had* killed a
very young and brave fighter named Patrick
O'Harrigan. Patrick's great talent was that he could
take an inhuman pounding. Darby's great talent was
that he could hit with either fist, as a hammer striking
an anvil. After that fight, neither man had ever fought
professionally again. Darby because he was sickened,
and O'Harrigan because he'd forever lost his dubious
talent.

But a man has to eat and Darby was accustomed to
eating well. In desperation, he'd accepted a job as a circus strongman. Like fighting, his job was to challenge

all comers to beat him for a prize. He'd lost only twice—once to a Bulgarian whose favorite delight was lifting a horse and carrying it into various drinking establishments, and another time to a towering German who could crumble rocks by squeezing either hand.

He'd traveled all over the world and had even performed before many of the nobility of the continent. It was during his fourth year that he'd begun to chronicle his travels. Soon, he'd started to sell stories. A few years later, he had tried his hand at writing a western dime novel and, with his usual dedication, he'd soon become a very successful writer. Now, Darby fought only in self-defense. However, he never allowed his strength to diminish, and he contented himself by lifting anything which presented a personal challenge. He stood 5 feet 9 inches and weighed 255 pounds.

Darby pushed back his chair and poured a small quantity of the best brandy to be found in Running Springs, Wyoming. "Blast," he muttered darkly. "Blast!"

Dolly Beavers, the owner of the Antelope Hotel and a robust and provocative woman, brushed her long blonde hair back and leaned forward with a look of concern.

"Come over here, Darby, and I'll soothe your ruffled feathers, though I have no idea why you should be upset. It was a very nice letter."

"Nice letter!"

Dolly blinked at the outburst with her lovely eyelashes. "My," she said, "you *are* upset. But why? Only last week you told me you were going. Remember how I cried?"

Just the thought of it, he saw, was threatening to disturb her all over again. Even now, her eyes were starting to glisten and there was a tremor on her lips.

"Now, Dolly. Please don't start it again."

She nodded bravely. "Oh, I won't. You're a writer and I know it's selfish of me to expect you to stay here in Running Springs. Go," she cried in anguish.

"I'd like to," he muttered. "Franklin is correct about the Pony Express being the greatest story now unfolding on the frontier."

He stood up and began to pace back and forth. "But don't you see," he said, "if I proceed West, they'll think it was *their* idea. And the next thing I know, Mr. Franklin, with all the best intentions, will be suggesting how I should actually *write* the story."

Darby shook his head in resignation. "No," he said quietly, "as much as I want to be a part of this great piece of history, I cannot."

Dolly Beavers looked at him steadily, her lips pursed in a way he knew meant she was in her deepest form of concentration. It didn't happen often. Generally, she simply blurted whatever was in her pure and uncomplicated mind. Sometimes the outcome was shocking, but generally it reflected the innocence of her thoughts. Dolly Beavers was the most guileless woman he'd ever known.

"If you don't go," she mused, "someone else will. Some other writer."

He stiffened. The thought of a lesser man doing the story made him wince as though in physical pain. "Let him," he said tightly. "Besides, there are plenty of other great stories I can choose from. Good stories, anyway."

"Such as?"

"Such as . . ." his voice trailed off and a silence lengthened. Flustered, he said, "Such as the big ore discoveries taking place around Virginia City."

"Virginia City?" A smile formed at the corners of her generous lips. "Why, Darby, that's right beside the Pony Express route and we both know it. How could you possibly be that near and avoid becoming involved in the Pony Express?"

"It's a matter of mental discipline."

"I see," There was a dubious expression on her face that he couldn't avoid noticing.

"Anyway," Darby grumbled, "the Pony Express is doomed. Already the telegraph is closing the gap across this country. No matter how resourceful and courageous the riders and officers of the Pony Express, horseflesh cannot compete with the telegraph."

"So it will all be gone," Dolly said, a trace of sadness in her voice. "How long?"

"I don't know," he admitted. "From what I've read so far, the Pony Express is in danger of not making even a single run. At best, the venture cannot survive more than two years."

Dolly rose from her seat on the bed, straightened her dress and moved over to the window to stand beside him. "Darby, if you did change your mind and decided to write the Pony Express story, would you have to be there the entire two years?"

"Of course not," he answered quickly. "It seems to me, the real juice in the tale would be how Russell, Majors, and Waddell are going to manage getting the undertaking off the ground, and the reasons why three sane and supposedly intelligent men would even try in the first place. I have to agree with Mr. Franklin when he writes that it is all based on the desperate hope of receiving the Central Overland mail contract."

"Quite a gamble."

"By heavens, it is at that!" Darby exclaimed. "Like most, I agree it is foolhardy but I have to admire their brass." He spun on his heel, absently smoothed the black coat and vest he always wore. "Yes, it *is* visionary. I wonder how they will do it. Is it possible?"

But Dolly wasn't listening. Apparently, her mind was fixed on other questions. "If you wouldn't have to be there the entire two years, how long?"

"How do I know?" he sighed absently. "It all depends on the stories I'd find. Most likely, I'd want to become acquainted with the riders themselves because, once it all begins, those men will become overnight heroes."

"That wouldn't take so long, less than a year, I'd think. And you wouldn't be in danger. I mean, you aren't thinking of doing any riding for them, are you?"

Darby laughed outright. "Dear woman. As you well know, my ineptitude in the saddle is already legendary; even your naïve question is a flattery. My involvement would be strictly as an observer."

"If only I could believe that. It's not that I don't trust you, but you said the very same thing before you became our sheriff when Zeb Cather was shot." At the memory, Dolly paled. "You were almost killed!"

"Won't happen again," he replied confidently. "Although I did do a pretty fair job of it, didn't I?"

"That's not the point. And later, on your last book, when you went mustanging in Nevada, I thought you a goner. You *were* shot, remember?"

"Of course," he said uneasily, "but . . ."

"And you'd promised before leaving me that you were only going to write about mustanging, *not* do it and wind up changing the whole scheme of things."

"I had to," he protested. "You know the story. It was an adventure of which I am most proud. We revolutionized the way mustangs are captured and saved thousands from senseless slaughter."

"I know," she said quietly. "Only every time you leave to write, you wind up getting shot or into fights. Things just happen to you."

Her face was so troubled. Darby took her into his arms. As always, the overpowering scent of her perfume made him almost giddy. It was so strong it killed insects at forty paces.

"Dolly," he wheezed, "this whole conversation is entirely pointless because I am not going anywhere."

Her reaction was uncharacteristic. First, she pulled away from his arms and then she said, "I think you're making a mistake. To allow someone else to write that great story seems very wrong to me. *Especially* if you promise you'd only be gone a few months and aren't thinking of trying to apply as a rider or some such thing."

"That's ridiculous. I weigh exactly *twice* what their riders will weigh. Besides, I refuse to discuss this any further. For a while, I shall relax and enjoy the fruits of my labors. Do nothing but enjoy what creature comforts I can find or have brought to this town. For six months at least."

"You will get as big as a house," she said. "And, when you're not writing, you become cranky."

Darby blanched. Big as a house. Cranky. "I will not," he spluttered. "But if that's what you fear, I'll remove myself from your hotel at once and find other accommodations."

"No, please. I apologize."

He was starting to grab his bags when her hand found his arm. "Darby, you're upset."

"Upset. Me. Upset. Why should I be upset?" he bellowed. "Just because you said I was cranky and getting fat? Well, let me tell you something, Dolly Beavers."

"Please do."

"I never get cranky," he stormed. "I have the mildest of dispositions, until I'm insulted. And as for getting fat . . . Buckinghams have always been robust. I don't even *like* thin people. They are almost chronically weak. Weak because they don't eat enough nor do they appreciate the benefits of lifting things to improve their strength and courage."

"You *are* terribly strong," she agreed. "The way you lift me and the bed so easily."

"Ha!" he cried. "I scarcely exert. I've never begun to press my limits."

"Oh, Derby," she cooed.

"Darby. When will you ever get my name right?"

He didn't wait for her answer. A hundred times he'd asked the same question and never received the same reply. "Get on the bed," he ordered. "And grab every scrap of furniture you can find in this room and pile it up around you."

"But . . ."

"Do as I say. You've grievously insulted me, woman. Big as a house. I'll show you."

Darby stripped down to the waist. His neck was as short and thick as a tree stump and his chest was as deep as that of a mustang pony. But there were no rippling muscles, no finely sculptured definition under his flesh. In fact, he looked as round and sleek as a walrus. Very deceptive. Only when his great strength was called to a test was the man transformed into a sight that rendered Dolly Beavers absolutely weak with admiration.

"The desk too?" she called, struggling to drag it across the room.

"Everything!"

Dolly nodded, her face deeply flushed. With more strength than some men, she hauled the desk over until it was against the bed and then toppled it onto the spread.

"That's all I can find," she panted.

At last, Darby turned from the window. His eyes surveyed the mound of furniture and trunks heaped nearly to the ceiling. Perhaps, he thought, his anger had gotten the better of him this time. What if he failed? Almost at once, he dispelled the thought and reinforced his purpose with the memory of her insult. He would show this woman.

"Climb up and hang on," he said.

She eyed the assemblage with open reluctance. "But where? There isn't room."

"Sit atop the trunk. I'll help you."

Once she was perched up there, the very legs of the four-poster bed trembled and seemed to bend and quiver.

"Darby, I'm scared," she wailed. "If you drop me, the whole mess is sure to plunge through the floor into my lobby."

"Then *I'm* the one who should be fearful," he gritted, sliding underneath. "At least you'll be on top. Now hang on."

With greater care than usual, he adjusted his hands in a very precise way. Of even more concern than the weight itself was the balancing required. If the load above shifted even just a little . . .

"Are you ready?" he called, taking deep breaths. "Because when I lift, it will have to come up fast."

There was genuine panic in her voice. "It's too much. Please . . ."

"Here we go." Darby's face was right against the bedsprings and, when he gathered his body and sent all his power into the lift, his neck contracted into his enormous shoulders. Every ounce of muscle he possessed went into his two massive arms—arms bigger than most men's legs. And slowly, very slowly, the bed began to shiver aloft. Inch by trembling inch, it rose. Dimly, he heard the woman above shouting, encouraging. But he couldn't understand her words, the blood was pounding in his head, and nothing mattered except the lift. Harder, more strength, more will.

Up, up, it came, tottering slightly, but still in balance. Just another inch or two; then his arms would be locked and he'd have it.

"Oh, Darby."

"Don't move."

Too late. The mighty arms never quite locked. The bed and the great mountain of weight began to shift. He was losing it.

"Jump!" he gasped as the weight dropped.

The foot of the bed struck first and the brass legs punctured the floor and stabbed to their hilt. Then the other pair snapped and Darby felt the whole works come down on him.

"Ahhh!" he bellowed, twisting sideways and heaving with his dying strength. Far, far away, he heard Dolly scream.

"No broken bones." the doctor said, shaking his head with wonder. "Mr. Buckingham, you are very lucky indeed. I don't understand why a man like you carries on so."

"Where's Dolly?" he growled. "Is she all right?"

"I'm fine, my dear."

Still woozy, he looked up at her. "I apologize."

She clasped his head to her ample bosom and he fought for air. "Don't apologize," she pleaded, "it was all my fault. I was the one who was trying to anger you into going to Nevada because I wanted you to do the Pony Express story. But no more. Your being unconscious made me realize I could never stay away from you."

He managed to get his forearm up and levered his mouth from her body. Air. Blessed air.

"And now," she was saying, "after coming so close to losing you, I realize we *must* be careful. We'll stay in your room. Be safe. Live off your royalties and my boarders. Just the two of us. And we'll get married."

"Oh, blast," he cried, his voice muffled as she leaned over him. Yes, he loved this woman, but not enough to be stifled to death. The very thought of them being confined together—and married—cleared his head in an instant.

"No!" he howled. "I *have* to go to Nevada. While I was out, it came to me in a dream. It's my destiny."

Dolly Beavers jerked back, her eyes both shocked and sad. "Do you mean it? Please tell me, my heart, you don't mean it."

"Oh, but I do," he swore, sitting up straight on the doctor's table. "The blow made me realize I was only being foolish and stubborn. I *can't* let someone else write that story."

Dolly whirled around, her back toward him, her face before a mirror. Over her shoulder, he saw her hands cover her face. She was taking it desperately hard.

"I'll come back," he promised. "Please understand."

When her hands dropped away, Darby's mouth also fell. Was that a faint smile? "I understand," she said in a trembling voice. "Oh, Derby, I will wait for you."

The woman didn't turn around but stood there, slumped and broken. Darby blinked twice. Yes, she *was* smiling, dammit.

Double blast, he muttered to himself. I do believe I've been taken. The shock was so great that he lay back down on the table and willed himself to sleep.

Less than two weeks later, Darby Buckingham arrived by stage in Carson City, Nevada, and promptly located the small Pony Express office. He was stiff and irritable from his long journey, but determined now to lay the groundwork for his next book.

While traveling from Salt Lake City, he'd come to realize the great obstacles that would beset the Pony Express. Across Nevada, the desert was more formidable than he possibly could have imagined. They'd covered stretches of land where nothing appeared to move except shimmering heatwaves over the dead alkali flats. Yet, he knew that wasn't true. This was hostile Indian country. How they managed to survive he could not even guess. But they were out there, waiting, watching. And, as they passed through that vast and sun-seared land, he noticed that the stage company employees wore strained and worried expressions. They never ceased to scan the still horizons, and their rifles were kept within arm's reach at all times. Darby found it

difficult to believe anything could be alive out there
and remain undetected. Yet, these men were clearly
concerned and he held his tongue.

More than once, though, he'd asked about the Pony
Express. He was met with blank looks or, when he explained its purpose, saw outright disbelief. Apparently,
though the enterprise was well known in the East, few
of these isolated men along the stage route knew anything of the events which were now taking place.

And so it was that, as he entered the small ram-
shackle offices in Carson City, he had grave doubts
about the Pony Express even having the capacity to
launch itself across the frontier, much less survive.

Inside the office, there was a small potbellied stove
in one corner and a pair of cluttered desks facing opposite walls. Piled in front of the rear door were a
saddle, bridle, and blankets. An ancient, almost tooth-
less dog thumped its hairless tail on the boards a few
times and settled into a fitful doze. Flies buzzed half-
heartedly around the room and an old clerk wearing a
green eyeshade blinked myopically at Darby as though
anyone entering the place was, in itself, a memorable
event.

Darby shook his head. This was supposed to be the
office of a man named Bolivar Roberts, who was in
charge of running the stations clear to Utah. Not too
auspicious.

"What can I do for you, Mister?"

"Are you in charge?" Darby asked skeptically.

"Of course not," the clerk answered, "I just keep the
books for Mr. Bolivar Roberts."

"My name is Darby Buckingham. I'd like to see Mr.
Roberts. Where can I find him?"

"He's busy. He's always busy. We all are."

Darby could have sworn the old fella stifled a yawn.
"Yes, I can see that," he said drily. "But I've come a
long way and . . ."

"Shhh! Don't move," the clerk hissed.

Darby froze. The man rolled up a piece of ledger
paper, then slowly raised it up. Whap! It slammed
down on the fly.

"Got 'em." He tipped the paper club up and said

solemnly, "Got 'em real good, too. Kinda messy, though."

"Yes," Darby said, "but, about Mr. Roberts?"

"Roberts? Oh, sure. He's out back in the corral looking at some more horses. That's what he's always doin', buyin' horses."

"Thanks," Darby said on his way out. "How will I recognize him?"

A twinkle came to the clerk's watery eyes. "He's the one walking on two legs, 'stead of four."

Darby ground his teeth and walked away from the receding laughter. Moments later, he was standing by the corral watching the men and horses.

"Bolivar," a tall, gaunt rancher was saying, "these are all first grade horses. I tell you there ain't any better around."

"Then," Roberts said, "the Pony Express is sure enough in trouble, 'cause *I* could outrun half these plugs."

He was a compact man about fifty years old with a tough and weathered appearance. From the moment Darby laid eyes on him, he sized Roberts up as a man more accustomed to physical work than shuffling papers. He was dressed like a freighter or stagehand, yet there was an unmistakable air of authority and competence about him.

Bolivar Roberts spat a stream of tobacco juice at the dust. "I told you, Jonathon, I want the best. Only the best, hear? There ain't but three horses I'd even consider."

"Three! Bolivar, every danged one of 'em is sound. They're the finest animals to be found in the entire Carson Valley."

"Is that right? Well then, I guess the Pony Express will have to go *outside* the valley, won't it."

The rancher kicked dirt. "Which ones do you like, damnit?"

"The two gray mares and the sorrel. Leave 'em in the corral and I'll have a rider take them for a hard run. If they stand up to it, can go a hard twenty-five miles, then I'll buy."

The rancher shook his head. "That's too far for any horse to go at a run. You'll kill 'em."

"Maybe," Roberts said. "But that's my orders and that's how it's going to be." He looked back at the horses. "Those three have mustang blood in them. I'd bet on it. I'll buy all you can find of that type."

The rancher's mouth tightened. "I don't know about lettin' you run 'em like that. If they go down, I'm out a hundred and fifty dollars."

Roberts laughed. A big, throaty laugh. "If even *one* of those mares has the bottom to go the distance, you've made two hundred dollars. It's your gamble, Jonathon. I've got my own to worry about."

"Cut 'em out, Buck," the rancher said after thinking it over. "We'll trail the others on to California next week."

"Good enough," Roberts said, turning away. "Just don't let me hear that you tried to sell them to my boss, William Finney. I mean that for a fact."

"Sure, sure. But I think you've underrated at least five of 'em."

"Which ones?" came the quick reply.

"The black with the white stockings."

"He's got white feet. They'll crack under hard conditions and he'd go lame no matter how good a job you did with shoeing him."

"Then how about the tall bay? His feet are sound."

"Narrow chested. He hasn't got the lungs for distance."

The rancher's jaw muscles tightened. "Then why didn't you like the buckskin? By God, he's got lungs!"

"Sure he does," Roberts nodded agreeably. "But he must weigh thirteen hundred pounds. Better suited to pulling a plow or maybe a stagecoach up these mountains than outrunning Indians. Hell, Jonathon, we both know he ain't fast. Unless I miss my guess, he's got a draft horse in his family."

"You don't miss a thing, do you?"

Bolivar Roberts grinned. He was a feisty appearing man with a likable face. "Can't afford to," he answered. "If just one of the horses I purchase goes lame, or quits, or can't keep the pace, it's not a rider's fault—it's mine. The very life of a relay rider depends on his mount, and that's why I'm paying four times the going price. I want the best animals money can buy. Go out and find me some more like the three I chose. I need 'em bad."

"Mr. Roberts," Darby said, stepping forward, "I'd like a few minutes of your time."

He'd been about to pass, but halted. Darby felt the man's eyes measure him and sensed the negative impression. It was always that way—at first—and Darby wasn't surprised. By his very manner of dress, he was instantly branded as an eastern city slicker, a dude. Furthermore, as he stood before the man in his starched white shirt, black suit, and round-toed shoes, he knew he presented a deceptively mild and soft appearance that was in sharp contrast to the rugged outdoors look of Bolivar Roberts.

To Darby, it was a price he had to pay. Yes, he was a dude and he claimed no particular competency at all when it came to riding, shooting straight, or throwing a loop. Yet, he was anything but soft underneath the few pounds of fat, and his courage had been more than tested up in Wyoming and in the mustang country of Nevada. Still, even as a slight frown gathered on Bolivar's face, Darby remained silent. Bragging was not his way, and all he could do now was hope that this man would give him a chance to explain.

"What can I do for you, Mister? I'm afraid my time is a little short these days."

He looked ready to leave at any second, so Darby came right to the point. "I'm a western writer," he said. "My name is Darby Buckingham. Perhaps you've heard of me?"

"No," Roberts replied. "I don't believe I have. Do you write those dime novels that have pictures of white stallions rearing up in the sky and fellas shooting pistols at the sun?"

"I have, but . . ."

"Mr. Buckingham. I'm not much of a reader myself. But once, I did pick up one of those things. The hero I read about was dressed in white pants and wore two guns backward, always mounted his 'stallion' by leaping over the back end of the thing, then . . ."

"Enough," Darby said stiffly. "You've made your point. I gather you don't think much of western dime-novelists."

"I don't think of them at all except as a joke," Roberts answered. "But if the people back East want to read that kind of tomfoolery, let 'em. Out here we don't have time for nonsense. Now, if you'll excuse me, I . . ."

"I'm not here to write about nonsense, Mr. Roberts. I came west more than a year ago to chronicle the true West. You ever hear the name of Zeb Cather?"

"Hell, yes. Who hasn't? He still alive?"

"He is. He saved my life, then I was able to return the favor. And, last fall, I wrote a story about mustanging up around Elko. There was a lot of trouble and, before it was over, a few men died."

"I heard something about that," Roberts said, the disapproval slipping out of his voice. "So, you're the Derby Man we read about in the *Carson Appeal.*"

Darby blushed. "Well, some people have called me that. My real name is Darby Buckingham. I used to write those kind of dime novels you were describing. Did very well with them, in fact. But, one day, I just couldn't do it anymore. No more fabrication and exploitation of my readership. So I came west and I've never regretted it."

He stopped, correcting himself. "That's not entirely true. I have regretted a few times that I've looked down a gunbarrel and wished I'd remained in New York."

"I'll bet," Roberts chuckled. "I've heard of you, all right. Got any books with you? I'd like to read one."

Darby smiled. "Of course. But, right now, I'm interested in *writing* one. I'm en route to Sacramento to do a book on the Pony Express."

"You don't have to go that far. Hell, it'll pass right through Carson City. Save yourself a trip over the mountains."

"Well, I'd kind of like to see it get started."

"Then you'll have to hurry," Roberts said, "and if

you really want to see it start, you'll need to go clear to San Francisco. That's where the big celebration begins."

"Why?" Darby asked. "I thought the Pony Express started in Sacramento."

"Technically, it does. From Sacramento, the mail will be carried aboard a river steamer to San Francisco. Going east, the same applies. Mail starts in San Francisco, goes upriver to Sacramento where the first rider jumps off toward the mountains. Here in Carson City, a few more letters will be added, then we strike out across the desert."

Darby glanced westward at the hovering Sierras. He'd heard about them. How the snow could pile sixty feet and more at the summits.

As if reading his thoughts, Roberts said, "Yep, they've got us all worried. Part of my job will be trying to keep those passes open in winter."

"At least," Darby said, "you won't have to concern yourself about that until fall. Surely, winter is over."

"Maybe. The snow is melting but there's still plenty up at the top. And this is only March. We've had heavy snow and blizzards as late as May. But likely you're right. Least we sure hope so."

Roberts frowned and deep worry lines rivered his mahogany-tanned face. "What with the Indians, Southern hell raisers, and that blasted desert out there . . . well, I just don't know."

"I've heard about the Indians and I've seen the desert, but what have the Southerners to do with your troubles?"

"You stick around for a few days and you'll find out. But don't stay too close," he warned. "I've had to fight my way out of trouble twice in the last week over this slavery issue and I wouldn't want to see you get hurt."

Darby felt slighted but didn't show his feelings. Besides, he *had* promised Dolly Beavers he'd stay out of trouble this time.

"You're a writer," Roberts was saying, "and perhaps you have seen some action out here. But I don't want to take the chance that you might get hurt on my account."

"It would help if you told me what the slavery issue has to do with the Pony Express. I'm afraid I don't understand."

The superintendent frowned and dug a circle in the dirt with the toe of his boot. When he glanced up, he appeared uncomfortable. "Mr. Buckingham, I'm a freighter and a westerner. Like most men, I came out to this country to find gold and maybe a better way of life. But, even so, we care about what's happening back East. Mr. Lincoln has his hands full on the slavery issue. Two years ago, in his house-divided speech, he warned this country that we were in great danger of being torn apart over the problem of slavery."

"That's true," Darby conceded, "and only last month, Jefferson Davis introduced an ultimatum resolution into the United States Senate demanding that Congress protect slavery throughout the western territories. He said the West was common property of all the states and hence open to Southern citizens who wanted to keep slaves." Darby's mustache bristled. "He also demanded the Northern states no longer interfere with the workings of the Fugitive Slave Act, repeal their personal liberty laws and respect the Dred Scott decision."

"That's correct," Roberts answered, "and anyone can see there's a showdown coming back there that will affect the history of this country."

"But, I'm not sure what it all has to do with the Pony Express."

"Listen, give me a few minutes to close up the office and we'll go have a drink. I'll tell you why the Pony has a lot to do with Southern and Northern interests."

As Darby waited, he tried to figure it out himself. In 1850, California had already joined the ranks of free states, so it seemed to him that issue was pretty well settled. True, the territories were not committed, but damned if he could figure out how a faster mail service would matter one way or another to North or South. Yet, as the minutes ticked by, he was sure Bolivar Roberts wouldn't make such a statement without basis in fact. He was eager to find out. It was a shame, he thought, with all the other problems the enterprise faced, that he should now discover one more.

Darby and Bolivar had barely settled down at a back table in the Nevada Saloon when a rowdy group of men entered and started demanding drinks at the bar.

"Damn," Roberts swore. "If they see me, there's going to be trouble."

Darby casually glanced around, then turned back. "Who are they?"

"Paid troublemakers. That great big one, his name is Claude Tulley and he's a bad man in a fist fight. The others are no better, and I've had warnings from old Clayton that the Pony Express will never complete a run."

Darby peeked back. Claude Tulley was easy to pick out. The man must have stood at least six and a half feet tall. His shirtsleeves were rolled up to his bulging biceps and he had dull, almost subhuman eyes set in under the heaviest brow of bone Darby had ever observed. He looked like the kind who would break your knuckles if you punched him in the face.

"The old one is the man that I worry about," Roberts said in a whisper. "He claims to be from the Deep South. I was told that they ran him out, and the Southern courts have his land tied up. He got into some kind of big trouble back there. The way I see it, Clayton thinks if he can stop me, he'll be able to call in some favors and get back his plantation."

"But what . . ."

"He's twisted," Roberts hissed. "When they ran him out of the South, something inside his head snapped. He vows he'll go back to redeem his honor."

"Are all six of the others on his payroll?"

"You might say that. They're a pack of misfits and opportunists. I hear that Clayton has promised them that if they help him kill the Pony Express, they'll all be rewarded by Jefferson Davis with land and slaves."

"That's preposterous!" Darby cried.

"Sure it is," Roberts agreed. "But you try and tell

them. Especially that Claude Tulley. He'll laugh and break you like the wishbone of a chicken."

Darby's outburst had sounded above the raucous noise along the bar. Suddenly, he realized the room was quiet.

"Hey," Claude boomed. "Shut up over there."

Bolivar Roberts whispered, "They still can't make me out. Turn around and ignore them."

Darby scowled and his mustache bristled. He glared back across the table. Roberts seemed to have sunk in his chair. "Are you afraid of them!"

"We're trapped, man. There's six of 'em and Claude Tulley all by hisself is enough for both of us."

Under Darby's eyes, he shifted uneasily. "I'm no coward but I'm not crazy, either. I can't run the Pony Express with my arms and legs broken."

It nearly killed Darby, but he could see Bolivar Roberts's point of view. If given the chance, the man would have a vital part of forming history. Besides, six to two were mean odds. "All right," he muttered, "but I'm not used to being told to shut up by anyone."

He poured another drink and downed it neat. A silence stretched between them until Darby grew weary of the background noise. "I'm tired, Bolivar," he said. "I just got off the stage and haven't even had a chance to find a room."

"Try the Baker House."

"Are you coming?"

Roberts took a deep breath. "No," he said finally, "I guess I'll stick."

"But they'll see you."

"Can't be helped." His jaw muscles tightened. "If Clayton sics Tulley on me, I'll go to my gun. No other choice."

Darby had started to rise, but changed his mind. "I won't leave you here," he said stubbornly.

"Yes, you will. It's me they'd like to bust up, not you."

For one of the very few times in his adult life, Darby wasn't quite sure what to do. He knew he wasn't going to leave this man, yet he didn't want to be responsible for what might happen to the local superintendent. Then, he saw Roberts stiffen.

"Well, well, look who's hiding in the corner." The old man laughed. "The very one whose task it is to spread Northern lies across the western territories. My boys, we are in luck today. Yes, suh."

Bolivar Roberts climbed to his feet and Darby followed. Clayton was smiling from ear to ear and it wasn't a nice smile at all.

"Claude, you see that? He was hiding back there all this time. Like a sneakin' little rat. Didn't even bother to say his hellos or anything."

"He still ain't," Claude said very seriously. "I don't think he likes us, Mr. Clayton."

"Hmm, you may be right. Maybe you should go over there and teach him some manners."

Claude beamed.

"You come over here," Darby warned, "and I'll put you down for the count. I mean it. Don't let that man talk you into getting hurt."

The giant actually hesitated. "Hold up, Claude. Maybe this . . . gentleman doesn't quite understand his predicament."

"Oh, I think I do," Darby said easily.

"We'll see, Mister. When a man butts into something bigger than himself, he has to pay a price."

Darby saw the other five men push off from the bar and felt the sweat begin to pop out from his body. The room seemed very hot all of a sudden.

"Mind if I take off my coat before I . . . pay the price?" he asked.

Clayton thought that was very funny. It took him almost a full minute to catch his breath. By the time he did, Darby had his coat off and his own sleeves rolled up tightly. He'd studied each of them one by one and judged them with a fighter's eye for both strength and quickness. Now, he knew exactly the order he would go after them if he got by Claude Tulley. And staring at the leering giant, he knew *that* was a pretty big if in itself.

Chapter 2

The outcome of the battle wasn't in question and everyone knew it. Especially Clayton, who seemed to find some pleasure in delay. Even more, he obviously wanted an audience. Perhaps, among the few strangers in the room, he hoped for fresh recruits. Whatever, he stated his views with venomous passion for all to hear.

"You're trying to put a spike through the heart of the South, Roberts. Don't think we don't understand what's going on. This is a scheme to take the mail out of Southern hands. You'd like to bypass all of us and ruin the Butterfield Stage Line."

"The Butterfield route should have been abandoned years ago," Roberts said hotly. "And it would have been, if it weren't for politics."

"That's not true! The Southern route is best for everyone. It avoids the mountain passes you propose to travel and . . ."

Roberts was angry and his voice quivered with it. "And it's a good thousand miles farther than the Central Overland. It makes no sense at all that our mail should be delivered by way of El Paso, Texas. By God, any fool can look at a map and see that."

"Are you calling me a fool?" came the quiet reply. "For if you are . . ."

"I'm not," Roberts said. "You're plenty smart, and out for personal gain. It doesn't take any brains to know that. What you want, Clayton, is a big piece of the South—for services rendered."

"What services?" he asked.

"Don't insult us," Roberts spat. "We all know there's a war brewin' and the South needs control of the mail. That way, it could isolate the Pacific Coast for months and give their sympathizers time to foment California's secession."

"Perhaps that wouldn't be such a bad idea."

"The people in California have made their choice. The South should respect that instead of attempting to control news from the East. Once that happened, they could flood us with one-sided journalism and intimidate the Unionists."

"Are you quite through, Mr. Roberts?"

Roberts ground his teeth in silence.

"Then it is my turn. We see what the North is trying to do by allowing you to experiment with this . . . this fool's gamble. It wants to bolster its sagging prestige, which holding the West would surely do. It wants California's gold and that of our own promising Comstock to use against the South."

"And you don't?" Roberts shouted. "Not only does the South want our minerals, but it would love to establish great cotton plantations in the rich California valleys, whose soils and climate are so much like your own. And why?" he scoffed. "To perpetuate slavery, that's why. And to serve as a western base that would turn back and absorb the entire southwest and northern Mexico. But I see through you, Mister. All this talk is just smoke because your interests aren't based on love of the South, and you're not working for Jefferson Davis—only for yourself. You're an opportunist and a charlatan. Your kind would trade sides in a minute if there was more to gain. And that's the part that turns my stomach. Why don't you tell your followers the truth—or can't you admit it even to yourself?"

Clayton was white with anger. His sunken cheeks twitched in fury. Watching him, Darby was sure the man was going to draw. But he didn't. At last, he seemed to will himself under control. His voice crackled like burning pine needles. "You're a liar," he breathed.

Bolivar Roberts's hand shaded his gun butt and Darby could almost feel the finger of death tracing its way through the still air.

"I have both of you gentlemen to thank for enlightening me about the stakes that are involved in the success or failure of the Pony Express. It's clear to me that you, Mr. Clayton, have as much reason to wish the enterprise to fail as Mr. Roberts here has to see it succeed. I say, let's put it to the test and let the gamble win or lose."

"And I say, you'd better stay out of this, stranger," Clayton rasped, never taking his eyes off Roberts.

"I can't," Darby said. "Because I'm a friend of Mr. Roberts and an admirer of President Lincoln." He *had* to divert either man from drawing in anger.

Clayton wrenched his attention to Darby. "Then you're a fool."

"Perhaps. But I'm not so foolish as to want to die over a matter that will be decided by forces greater than ourselves. I say let's settle our differences with our fists. I'm sure your trained giant would agree."

Claude Tulley showed he wasn't totally dull. "Yep, I sure would," he said, grinning with anticipation. "I'd like that real good."

"How about it, Clayton? I'm not armed and it might be difficult to explain how the seven of you found it necessary to resort to killing."

The old man wanted Roberts dead. He tasted blood and he wanted it. Darby could see him struggling between reason and desire. Fortunately, reason won out.

"Perhaps we ought to pound sense into your Yankee-lovin' skulls."

"You can try," Darby said, feeling a great measure of relief. If he survived this, from now on, he was at least going to carry his derringer.

Clayton leaned back on the bar and casually poured a glassful. "Do a good job of it, boys. But have fun."

It was Darby's opinion that fights were usually won or lost during the first two seconds. Or with the first punch. To win, the formula was brutally simple—you hit fast and you hit hard, with no backward steps and absolutely no hesitation. Above all, even if you were badly overmatched and outnumbered, you never showed fear. Nothing gave an opponent more of an edge than the awareness of fear. Again and again, he'd seen this principle tested and proven true. He'd observed it even in dog fights, where the sheer ferocity of an inferior animal brought it victory when victory seemed impossible.

So it was that he neither considered the odds nor the consequences. Like a cannon shot, he hurled himself at Claude Tulley. Take out the strongest and sometimes the others would lose their stomach for the fight. In the moment before closing, he saw a flicker of alarm in the giant's face. Perhaps, because of his extraordinary size, Tulley wasn't accustomed to being singled out for attack. Whatever, before he quite realized it, Darby's fist blurred through the air, sliced between Tulley's upraised guard, and exploded against the jawbone. One of Darby's knuckles cracked and pain jolted up his arm. But he ignored it. When Tulley's mouth flew open, Darby pounded an uppercut to the stomach and Tulley pitched over face first, gasping for air like a beached whale.

So much for the element of surprise. Before Darby could pivot about, he felt an arm lock on his neck and jerk him around. Then, a fist swept into his vision and the entire left side of his face went numb.

Darby chopped his elbow back into a stomach and the stranglehold broke. He spun around and sent two blows into the man's face, only to have someone bash him in the jaw so hard that he went reeling sideways. He tripped over a fallen chair and two men came crashing down on top of him, punching furiously. His head slammed down against the floor and Darby's eyes lost focus.

Blindly, he kicked out and heard a cry as he rolled sideways, just as a pair of boots stomped where his chest should have been. He was halfway up when someone tackled him in the back and the air blasted out of his lungs.

"Darby, help," Roberts yelled.

"Help," he raged. "How can I . . ."

A fist grazed his cheek, taking a stinging hunk of flesh. Darby managed to get his thick legs under him and up he came with someone on his back. He lowered his shoulders and charged at the three men who were swarming all over Roberts. When he hit that mass of bodies, they went over like dominoes and he was on top.

From that second on, he never gave them a chance. Two heads came up and he grabbed them by the hair and cracked their skulls together like a pair of eggs. They slumped, not to move again. He'd forgotten the man on his back until the fellow started spurring him, bashing his ears so hard they rang. Darby stormed up and pitched over backward, landing his full weight on the unfortunate rider whose shriek hit an incredibly high note and then changed into an altogether different sound—more like a wounded grunting.

Out of the corner of his eye, Darby saw Roberts desperately trying to push himself erect. One of the superintendent's eyes was already swollen nearly shut and his lips were smashed. "Stay down," the writer gritted, "or . . ."

He never finished. He was half-crouched and off balance when something struck him in the back of the head so hard that lights flashed behind his eyes, and it felt as if a thousand fiery needles seared his brain.

Darby pitched to the floor and, dimly, he saw the behemoth looming over him with a gun in his hand. Then he heard it cock.

"Claude, no!"

The giant shuffled around and Darby tried to reach out and grab his boot. But he couldn't. His arms were leaden, his fingers quivering.

"Claude, he's unarmed. If you kill him, it will be murder."

Ten seconds passed and they seemed like ten years as Claude Tulley held the gun and waited while his great chest heaved and his small mind groped for its decision.

"He hit me before I was ready. I owe him." Claude kicked out, and Darby winced with pain as the boot lanced into his ribs.

"Get up, dude. I don't need the gun. This time, I'm ready."

To prove his point, he shoved it into his holster.

Darby blinked, trying to clear the pain that made his eyes watery and his head spin. He didn't think he *could* get up, much less fight. His hair was sticky and warm, and he knew he'd been pistol-whipped hard.

"Can't you see he's done." Tables crashed and Darby thought he saw Roberts trying to stand. "You touch him again, so help me, I'll . . ."

"Shut up," Clayton raged. He walked over to Darby, and actually leaned over to peer in his face. "Have you had enough, city slicker? You learned better'n to butt into something that don't concern the likes of you? Huh?"

Darby's head rolled sideways, back and forth, and the old man chuckled. "Stand him up, Cedrick. Stand him up tall."

A pair of powerful hands gripped Darby by the shirt and reared him upright. He staggered and tried to grab at Claude, but his reactions were gone. The giant slipped away and, as Darby staggered, Claude Tulley had his moment. The blow was measured and delivered with a killing force. In Darby's condition, it was almost merciful.

It took nearly three days before Darby could chew his food and, during that time, he rested and thought about what was to come. He also changed his mind about going over the Sierras to Sacramento. The Pony Express would go through Carson City and, sooner or later, so would Claude Tulley.

That his jaw hadn't been broken or his head cracked by Tulley was something of a miracle. Never, in all his years of fighting, had he been dealt such blows. The fact that he was still alive was proof he possessed the constitution of a horse. That Claude Tulley had been able to recover from Darby's first two punches was also proof that the giant could take a beating. Darby stored that knowledge deep inside for future use. Again and again, he tested the cracked knuckle and willed it to heal before Tulley returned. But whether it did or not changed nothing. He'd been pistol-whipped and knocked senseless.

On the fourth day, he walked over to a nearby livery stable where he found some kegs of rusting horseshoes.

And, out behind the barn where no one could see, he began to lift his weights. Yes. He *would* be ready.

"Darby," Bolivar Roberts said, "What's wrong? You haven't been by the office. I've finished horse buying and just got word from Mr. Russell to start hiring riders."

"That's good," Darby said, placing almost three hundred pounds of horseshoes down. "Have you heard any news about Clayton and Tulley?"

The Pony Express superintendent's mouth crimped down at the corners. His lips were still caked with blood. "No, I haven't," he said quietly. "I think they've done what they wanted to do. The doctor said these cracked ribs of mine should keep me in bed for at least two weeks."

"How's the arm?" Darby asked, looking down at the sling.

"Oh, they broke it all right. When Tulley hit you that last time, I went for my gun. One of 'em pinned me from behind and another smashed my wrist and hand with his gun butt."

Bolivar's fingers were swollen and purplish and Darby swore silently.

"Now, don't take it so hard," Bolivar said. "Our day will come around and things will be different."

"They sure will." Darby shook his head. "But I guess they've brought things to a standstill for now."

"How do you figure?"

"You've got those stations to set up east of here. As long as you can't ride . . ."

"Hell," Bolivar swore, "it was the doc said that. Not me. Why, I been busted up worse on the bucking string and went right on with my work."

"You mean you'll still be riding out?"

"Got to. No one else I trust. My boss, Mr. Finney, has his hands full over on the other side of this mountain. Now, I've got work to do," he grinned, "and if you're still set on writing that book, then so do you. How about it, Buckingham? Are you a writer or a lifter? You want to write this piece of history or stay out here behind the barn sulking with revenge and building muscles?"

Darby swallowed, then sauntered over to retrieve his shirt. His biceps, pumped up by the exertion, measured over twenty-two inches and he had to squeeze them in through his sleeves. "I'm a writer first," he said. "And I do recall reading your newspaper ad a few days ago advertising for riders. Wasn't the meeting today?"

"This very hour, my friend. That's why I hunted you down. I've got to stop by my office. Why don't you go on over. I promise, you'll find it interesting."

Darby finished buttoning his white shirt. He shrugged into his coat and fitted his derby at the desired angle. "Bolivar," he said as they were leaving, "you've reminded me of my responsibilities by carrying out your own. I'll be waiting. Thank you."

The man blushed. "Just thinking of my own skin, Darby. One of these days, we'll be hearing from Clayton again, and when we do I want you by my side."

"I will be. That's a promise gladly kept," Darby whispered. *Never,* he thought, had a promise been so anticipated.

Darby stood at the rear of the hall and studied the crowd that waited. What an assemblage! Two hundred men at least, from every imaginable walk of life. Gamblers, cowboys, clerks, prospectors, and a smattering of grizzled old Indian fighters and buffalo hunters. There were nervous, pink-cheeked boys who tried to stand taller than they were, and at least ten men with the look of professional gunslingers kept their backs to the walls.

Everyone was keyed up with anticipation but, generally, the crowd was quiet. A few latecomers, upon sticking their heads in the door of the hall, sized up the competition and sadly slipped away. No one knew for sure how many riders and hostlers Bolivar was going to hire, but it was certain to be not all of them.

"Say, Mister," a young cowboy said, cocking back his hat and smiling good naturedly.

"Yes?"

"I mean no offense but I can tell you right now you're wasting your time here."

Darby remained silent and the man shifted uncomfortably. "The truth of the fact is," he said, his face growing serious, "I've heard they're going to hire only lightweight gents like myself. And, Mister, you're the biggest man in the hall."

"Perhaps, I'm looking for a job as a hostler," Darby suggested with amusement.

"You?" The man suppressed a laugh. "If you're a hostler, then I'm President Abraham Lincoln. No sir, just the way you're dressed would tell anyone but a fool that you've come in from the East. And with that derby hat and fancy suit, well . . ." his voice trailed off.

Darby fought down an urge to tell this brash young upstart that although he *was* from the East, he'd been living in Wyoming lately. Furthermore, after mustanging in Nevada . . .

"My name is Warren Upson, Sir. And I've got to be a Pony Express rider. There's nothing in this world I want more."

"You sound quite serious about that."

"I am. You may think me young, but I've had some experience. My father," he said proudly, "is editor of the *Sacramento Union*. He wanted me to take over the paper someday, but I'd have no part of it."

"Journalism is a fine profession," Darby retorted.

"Not for me. Up until yesterday, I was working up in those Comstock mines. But I quit to be a rider."

Darby frowned. He knew that the competition for riders was going to be stiff. And this man seemed so young—almost a boy. In spite of himself, Darby hoped young Upson didn't get the job. Too dangerous for a lad his age.

"The vaqueros taught me how to ride," he was saying. "I ain't bragging when I say I became good enough to beat my teachers at some of them rodeos. And I can hit a squirrel off a running horse six times out of six."

"That sounds pretty difficult."

"Oh," the young man smiled. "It's not so tough." He grew serious. "I never expected there'd be so many fellas here today. Do you suppose this Mr. Roberts will hire me?"

The young fellow looked so worried Darby had to give encouragement. "Maybe so. He needs good men and if you can ride and shoot as well as you say, well . . ."

"There's something else he should know. I've roamed the Sierras all the time I was growing. I understand her moods. In the worst blizzard, when you can't see a foot in front of your nose, I could find my way through. I know every pass and valley, where the avalanches fall and . . ."

"Take it easy!" Darby said. "Why don't you save this for Mr. Roberts?"

Warren Upson grinned. "Oh, I will, if given the chance. But, from the size of this crowd, I may not have time. The reason I'm telling you all of this, Mr. Buckingham, is that I asked around last night and learned you're Mr. Roberts's friend. So, if I don't get the chance to say my piece, put in a word for me, will you?"

Darby frowned. Here he'd been thinking that this young man was just a compulsive talker, and all the time he'd known exactly what he was doing.

"I'll tell him," Darby said grudgingly.

Upson grabbed his hand and began pumping it. "Thanks plenty. I'm grateful. Be sure to tell him about my knowing those Sierras. You see, I'll ride wherever he puts me, but I'd most prefer those mountains. They're the real enemy we face. If I beat them, it'll be history. I want to be the first rider going east over those great mountains and I'm the only one who can do it."

The boy walked away after telling Darby how to spell his name correctly so that he got it right in his book. Darby shook his head. Remarkable young fellow—bold, earnest, intelligent, and apparently well-qualified. He reached inside his coat and retrieved a tablet of paper and a pencil. Warren Upson, he scribbled. He'd remember.

All at once, a hush fell over the crowd and they parted for Bolivar Roberts. Darby hardly recognized the superintendent. He wore a suit and white shirt with a starched collar. His Stetson looked as if it had come right out of the box. Even with a black eye and swollen lips, he looked important.

Bolivar climbed up on the speakers platform and looked out at the sea of faces. He beamed.

"My friends, when I placed that little ad in the paper, I never expected, never dared hope, for such a response. It is damned fine to see the spirit of adventure is still burning in the hearts of the West's finest. And adventure, my friends, as well as an honorable wage," he added quickly, "is what I'm here to talk about. My name is Bolivar Roberts. I'm the local superintendent in charge of the Pony Express between here and Roberts Creek Station. I work for Mr. William Finney, and he takes his orders directly from Russell, Majors, and Waddell."

"We've heard of them last three," an old, buckskin clad fellow called. "You're the one we ain't sure about."

"Sometimes I'm not sure about myself, friend," Bolivar admitted with a smile that brought laughter among the onlookers and evaporated the tension.

Darby nodded with approval. He'd been out West long enough to know that men on the frontier appreciated humor and disliked anyone who couldn't take ribbing or being joked with. He was seeing a new side of Bolivar Roberts. A quality, he believed, that would prove his employers had made an excellent choice.

When the laughter died, Roberts's face grew serious. "I recognize at least half of you, and I understand there's quite a few who rode all the way over from California. As I said a minute ago, I appreciate that. But, I'm afraid we won't be able to hire even half the number in this room." There was a low rumble of disappointment.

"To begin with, I think I ought to tell you some background—why the Pony Express was conceived. As you know, the California Gold Rush in forty-nine . . ."

A square-jawed, muscular young cowboy with a brash expression hollered through a pair of cupped hands. "Never mind the history lecture, Mr. Roberts. All we care about is ridin'."

The superintendent's expression hardened and his eyes came to rest on the caller. "What's your name?"

"Bob Haslam," came a quick and confident reply. "I'm a crack shot with pistol or rifle and I can stick a saddle longer than any man in this room."

It was a moment before Roberts spoke but, when he did, his voice was cool and hard. "I believe that, Mr. Haslam. I truly do. But you're wasting time here. Any man who can't listen—or won't—has no place with the Pony Express. Thanks for coming."

The cowboy flushed deeply and glanced around at some of his friends who suddenly appeared to have taken a sharp interest in the condition of their boots. Haslam was struggling with his pride and Darby could almost see him weighing the decision, whether to leave or eat crow and apologize.

"Reckon I learn fast," he said after a long pause. "A touch of history never hurt anyone, Mr. Roberts."

"Glad to hear you say that, young man. How old are you?"

"Twenty."

"How much do you weigh?"

Haslam frowned. "I don't know. Maybe 135 pounds."

"Lose five pounds and if you can do what you say, I'll hire you."

"Yes, sir!"

Bolivar Roberts turned his attention back to the crowd. "Most of you are either too big or too old," he said quietly. "I've got orders to hire men who are between the ages of nineteen and twenty-five. The riders have to be light—under 135 pounds. And, most of all, they must be as tough as the country they'll face."

Several oaths were clearly heard from men who were too old, young, or heavy.

"On top of that, the riders have to be able to read and write, have a working experience with horses and be of sound moral character."

"Jumpin' Jehosophat!" a man called, "what's that supposed to mean?"

"It means," Roberts said, "no swearing while on the payroll. No gambling and no drinking."

A lot of the men who obviously did not fit the physical requirements had started for the door and Roberts yelled, "Hold up, folks! Everything I've said applies to both riders and hostlers *except* the weight and age. If any of you men can't be riders but still want to be a part of history making, I want you to apply for the hostler's jobs. The pay is the same only the risks aren't as great."

Several of those who'd started to file out returned. "What do the hostlers do?" one of them called.

"They have the horses saddled and ready for each relay rider," Roberts responded. "That's their main job. But they've also got to cook, haul water, shoe horses, and fight off Indians, if need be. They're damned critical to this whole operation. No matter what, they have to keep the stations open."

"What's the pay?"

"Fifty dollars a month and food. Later, we'll raise it."

"They're paying four dollars a day up in the Comstock mines," someone protested. "That's almost twice what you're offering."

"Then take it," Roberts ordered. "And by the time you pay for grub and whiskey at Virginia City prices, you won't have enough left to post a letter with our company. Besides, I always thought man was made to work up in the sunlight and fresh air instead of like a damned prairie dog in the dirt. But that's your decision and I respect it. I won't hire a man who is dissatisfied with the pay. Because, if I do, and the goin' gets hard out there, he'll quit."

This, Darby knew, was a point that was of great concern to Bolivar Roberts. More than once, the man had brought up the subject. Loyalty, he'd said, was critical. The hostler and riders would be exposed to danger every day they were on the job. They'd be in Indian country and too far from civilization to seek help. So they'd have to go it alone—maybe die alone if that's what was necessary. Quitters just wouldn't do. It would be tempting and too easy for a man to just saddle up one of the Pony Express horses and ride away to safety. Bolivar hadn't told the men this, but

Darby knew the company had established a policy to track down and see that any such horse thieves were brought to trial before hanging.

No one wanted to see that happen. That's why Bolivar had to choose his men right the first time. They *had* to be loyal and in this for more than the money. As he thought about this, he realized Bolivar had returned to his history lesson.

"Most of us came to the West to find land or gold. Mostly gold in California. When we arrived a decade ago, California was wide open country except for a few big ranches, and San Francisco was no more than a collection of shacks and waterfront shipping warehouses. Up in the Sierras, there were grizzly and a few tribes of peaceable Indians. Things moved slow in those days."

He paused. "But the gold changed all of that, and it changed the whole destiny of the Union. In just two years, more than a hundred thousand men and some mighty brave women came racing across the prairie determined to make their fortunes. And some died of thirst trying to cross the Humbolt basin or froze in the Sierras or maybe—God help them—were scalped by the Indians.

"However they came, they suffered across the same God-forsaken lands the Pony Express intends to go through. And just like those before us—we're *going* to make it. Only faster. Faster than any man dared dream. But it's not going to be easy. Not a damn bit."

"We know the risks," a beefy freighter shouted. "And none of us is scared."

"Of course you aren't," Roberts answered. "And what's more, you know how to stick when the going gets tough or none of you would be here today. When the gold was squeezed out of these mountains, thousands returned to the East, but you boys stayed out West to build a nation. It was hard; the cold, the desert heat, the lack of supplies, and all the comforts you left back there."

Amen, Darby thought, remembering New York steaks, Cognac, and Broadway theaters he missed so badly.

"But do you know what I remember being the greatest disappointment of all?" Roberts asked.

"The women!" a man yelled. "There weren't any. Still aren't many, to speak of." Men laughed.

"Naw, it was the whiskey," someone else shouted. "I haven't had a decent drink since I left Philadelphia twelve years ago."

"Couldn't prove it by me, partner. Sure hasn't slowed you down none." More guffaws.

Bolivar held his hands up for silence. "Women and whiskey are in short supply. I admit that. But think about it. What was the biggest day of celebration in the mining camps?" Without waiting for an answer, he told them. "It was the day the mail arrived. Because we were Yankees, southerners, eastern farmers, or city clerks. That's where we came from and that was our home. We left our wives, sweethearts, and old folks to blaze a trail. Some of us found gold and all of us knew loneliness."

The men nodded. One fellow spoke up, "Mr. Roberts, I remember I never got letters, but the boys would all pass around theirs for everyone to read."

"Yeah, and I paid ten dollars in gold for a *New York Tribune* newspaper that was six months old and had almost all the ink wore off from being owned by so many," said another.

Bolivar nodded. "Back in those days, the mail was what kept us all going from day to day. A single letter from someone loved back home made strong men cry right out in the open. The mail, friends, gave us hope and kept us pushing on, just as sure as the meat and whiskey we took inside."

He stopped, scanned the eager faces, and his voice dropped so low that the listeners bent forward, the better to hear. "And I'll tell you something: the mail still gives us hope and courage and strength. Is that true?"

Every man in the room nodded vigorously and Darby was strangely moved. It was a thing he'd never considered, but the way Bolivar put it made him realize how important the mail really was. Back East, it was taken almost for granted. Out here, it was a precious service indeed. Darby shook his head thoughtfully.

He'd learned an awful lot about the Pony Express since arriving in Carson City. And it hadn't even begun yet. One thing was certain—Bolivar Roberts was quite a man. He had a way of speaking out that stirred listeners, making them think of things greater than themselves. Darby's respect for the superintendent continued to grow.

"Remember how long it used to take for mail to reach us? Six months around Cape Horn. Later, when they put steamers on both sides of Panama, we were almighty pleased to get it in just one or two months. Now, the Butterfield Stage boasts about its twenty-five day schedule, and we are grateful, even though a few people wonder why our mail has to go clear down through Texas and Arizona first."

"That ain't so bad," offered a man with a distinctive southern drawl.

Darby tensed. The last thing Bolivar wanted now was a political confrontation. But the superintendent skirted the danger like a lifetime politician.

"No, it isn't," he said easily. "The Butterfield has a fine reputation. But, gentlemen, the people I work for believe we deserve our mail as fast as is humanly possible. News of home and news of the great events back East."

Darby's interest was at its peak. So far, very few men knew the schedule. Back East, they didn't believe it. Would these men?

"How fast, Mr. Roberts?"

Bolivar smiled, hesitating for effect. "Russell, Majors, and Waddell, owners of this nation's most successful and prominent stage line, think you ought to get your mail . . . in *ten* days."

They were thunderstruck. Mouths flew open, then closed with the words *ten days* on everyone's lips.

"You heard me right. Ten days." He shrugged. "Reckon I understand those stares I see on your faces. Mine probably looked the same when I first heard the schedule. But that's it."

He pointed across the room to Darby. "That big fella back there isn't applying as a rider, should you be wondering." Everyone turned and Darby nodded.

"He's a writer and he's in Carson City to help set the history books straight. Don't anyone laugh or he's liable to flatten you, but up in Wyoming, they call him the Derby Man. You fellas call him Sir. We'll be up in my hotel room after this and those men who still want to sign up as riders or hostlers can line up outside the door and we'll talk to you one at a time."

Bolivar started to leave, then halted. "There's just one thing you boys have to know. Any man who signs on better be sure. I'll have no deserters or quitters. We got the best horses money can buy, but no matter how far or fast they can run, it wouldn't be enough to keep us from tracking a horse thief down and stringing him from a tree. No threat," he said, walking out, "just a fact you all should know."

Over the next three days, they'd interviewed more than a hundred men and Darby gathered a lifetime's worth of material for his western stories. It became apparent that Bolivar Roberts was most interested in men with character as well as toughness. Those who swaggered into the room with guns tied to their legs, he dismissed at once. He didn't want riders who favored a scrap. They'd have the fastest horses in the country, grain-fed runners who could easily outdistance the wiry, grass-eating Indian ponies. Speed was to be their greatest weapon, and the riders were always to remember that.

In fact, everything depended upon speed, and that was the reason some top riders, weighing over 130 pounds, were regretfully excluded. All aspects of the enterprise had been planned with swiftness in mind. Even the saddles were going to be stripped-down affairs over which a leather rectangle called a mochila was transferred from one horse to another. The mochila, with its four-locked pouches or cantinas, could be yanked off one horse and slipped over another bare saddle in far less than the two minutes allowed. Even better, the whole thing weighed less than thirteen pounds.

By the time the third day was over, both Darby and Bolivar Roberts were satisfied they'd picked the best

men for the job—men like the Sierra-wise Warren Upson and the fearless Bob Haslam. Men who would
stick when quitting seemed easier.

Bolivar Roberts passed out small, leather-bound
Bibles to every one of them. "This is the last step," he
said, "before we get started. Mr. Alexander Majors
wrote this oath and every employee of this company
will swear to abide by it and sign his name to stand.
Before you do, I'll read it aloud for all to hear. Anyone
who can't live by it might as well leave."

I do hereby swear before the great and living God that
during my engagement, and while I am an employee of
Russell, Majors, and Waddell, I will under no circumstances use profane language; that I will drink no intoxicat-
ing liquors; that I will not quarrel or fight with other employees of the firm, and that in every respect I will con-
duct myself honestly, be faithful to my duties, and so
direct all my acts as to win the confidence of my employers. So help me God.

Not a man in the hall walked out. They made the
pledge—every one of them. Watching them sign, a
lump grew in Darby's throat. Crazy, but he almost
wished he could sign himself.

When it was over, Bolivar nodded stiffly and his
voice came out thick with emotion. "Gentlemen, we've
got a big job ahead of us. In the next few weeks, we'll
be building relay stations halfway across Nevada. Everything is ready. We leave tomorrow, but your pay
starts right now. With God's help, we *will* triumph!
You are dismissed."

Chapter 3

Establishing the chain of relay stations under Bolivar Roberts's jurisdiction was hard work. Along with William Finney, they'd rolled out of Carson City with a caravan of horses and wagons.

Darby realized at once that he'd vastly underestimated the size and complexity of the operation. Every wagon was heavily loaded with building materials, food, saddles and harnesses, horseshoes and anvils, and grain—plenty of grain—for those fast-running horses. Bolivar and Finney agreed that grain-fed mounts would have the heart and stamina to outrun the fleetest Indian pony.

Their first station was erected at Dayton, a pleasant enough spot on the Carson River. They felled some cottonwoods and worked up a quick lean-to. Then, leaving a couple of men and a few pounds of provisions, they pushed on toward the east.

After they left the Carson River, Darby began to wonder how the riders and hostlers would ever survive an Indian attack if one should come. The stations were not picked on the basis of defensibility. Not at all. As far as Bolivar and Finney were concerned, site selection was just a matter of being exactly twenty-five miles from the last camp, not a hundred yards more or less, no matter what.

It made Darby scowl with disapproval and some of the stationmasters justifiably angry. But that's where they put them because those were the orders coming from headquarters.

At the Sink of the Carson River, at Sand Springs, and at Cold Springs, it was decided to build the stations of adobe brick. They worked hard, and Darby was amazed at how strong the adobe became after it dried. If there was Indian trouble, there would be at least three fortresses which Pony Express employees could defend. Even the roofs were layered with the fireproof adobe.

But most of the stations were primitive at best. Later, the stationmasters would no doubt improve them, but initially they were just tents or a hole dug out of a hillside and lined with brush.

Time was running out and Darby couldn't help feeling sorry for the men they left behind to make do as best they could. As the caravans rolled further east, Darby would look back to see a couple of gents standing in the middle of the desert, likely as not miles from water and without a piece of shade or greenery in sight. Maybe they'd be sitting on a water barrel or trying to erect a flimsy canvas tent. There was no need to store the food and supplies because there really wasn't any place to put it.

One of the first tasks generally undertaken was the construction of a corral for the horses; one of the wagons had been filled with posts for that very reason.

It took them almost two weeks to go all the way to Robert's Creek, nearly three hundred miles from Carson City. By that time, Darby guessed he'd seen enough of the Nevada desert to last a lifetime. He was out of Cuban cigars and ready to return to civilization.

Bolivar Roberts must have felt the same way because they pushed the nearly empty wagons hard as they began the long return trip. Approaching each station once again, Darby was amazed at the progress that had been made. In many places, the Pony Express employees had ridden into the low ranges of mountains and cut wood. Pole shacks were up and, at some, the gaps between the slender logs were being filled in with either adobe or tightly packed brush. In one camp, Darby squeezed back into a tunnel and was astonished to find a small room with a tent-covered floor and candles flickering. When his eyes adjusted to the dim light, he saw a low table and a fireplace, complete with an air vent. At another station, the new occupants proudly displayed a perfect example of how to build a rock house.

"Ingenious, very ingenious," Darby said each time they bid farewell to another station.

"They'd better be," Finney replied. "Every one of them has his job cut out. Even if there's no Indian trouble at all, it won't be easy. Sometimes supplies will be late, or their water sources will start drying up as the days get hotter. They'll have to catch their own fresh meat and, in the winter, try to keep from freezing at night."

"They can do all those things," Bolivar said.

Finney looked up. They were almost at the end of their trip and ahead was Churchill Station. "I hope they live to get the chance to prove their worth, gentlemen."

Darby's head snapped around and followed Finney's gaze. What he saw made his stomach knot and the hairs on the back of his neck stand up and prickle.

Indians.

"Go easy," Bolivar ordered. "Pass it down the line of wagons. Nobody grabs a rifle unless I do first."

When the two managers stepped down from the lead wagon and advanced, Darby went along, too. But his heart was beating like a big war drum.

"Move slow," Bolivar Roberts warned. "That's young Numaga up there and, up to now, he's been friendly."

"I hope he is still," Darby whispered.

"So do I. If we can keep him happy, it will save a lot of bloodletting. If not . . ." His voice trailed away and not a man among them had a doubt what went unspoken.

Bolivar waved at the band and gestured for them to come forward. It was almost a full minute before the Indians even acknowledged his greeting.

"He's usually more friendly than that," Bolivar said worriedly. "We'd better shake out some supplies."

"Is Numaga the big one in the center? He's a giant."

"Yeah. He's impressive, all right. Every time I see him, I get to feeling helpless and weak as a child. He's even bigger than you are."

"Taller. Not bigger."

"Wait until he speaks. You're in for the surprise of your life."

"If I live through this, I will indeed appreciate it, Bolivar."

Finney was obviously not as familiar with the Paiute chief. "Bolivar, you don't think something is wrong, do you?"

"I'm not sure. But if there is, it's best we get it settled now. He's got at least twenty braves with him. It would be damned easy for him to follow our tracks east and wipe out every station on our line. We've *got* to work with Numaga. He's the one who decides whether the Pony Express succeeds or fails."

Darby couldn't take his eyes off the chief. The Paiute was an awesome figure. Tall and wide-shouldered, he was heavily muscled and lean in the waist. His legs were sinewy and powerful. He was dressed in a light doeskin jacket and pants. Around his neck was an animal-tooth necklace, and there was an orange tassle braided into his hair along the left side of his wide forehead. Everything about the man was broad. Prominent cheekbones dominated Numaga's face. His nose was flat and his nostrils seemed distended. It was a face the description of which his eastern readers would love, yet it lacked cruelty, and one look into those penetrating eyes was enough to tell Darby the chief had seen much of life and had learned things few would ever know.

As a man of equal strength and proportion, and as a writer who had discovered something new and dangerous, yet fascinating, he wished he could interview this man. But that, of course, was impossible. For one thing, it would demand an interpreter and, besides, the main concern was the Pony Express, not his sharp curiosity.

Then, the Paiute chief's eyes came to rest on Darby and the writer felt as though he were being measured. Height, 5 feet 9 inches; weight, 255; strength, enormous; quickness, superior; endurance, inferior.

"Greetings, Chief Numaga," Bolivar said with a bow. "It is good to see you again."

Numaga's lip curled. "You're a poor liar, Mr. Roberts, very poor."

Darby nearly fell over. The Indian chief spoke better English than most white men.

"Numaga, we *are* glad to see you," Finney said.

"Who is he?"

"My boss, Mr. William Finney."

Numaga nodded. "Why are you glad to see me, Mr. Finney?"

"Because we want to cross this land in peace."

"Why," the chief said, "is it always what *you* want. Never the Indian."

Finney blushed and Bolivar stepped in. "We know you also want peace; that's why we are confused and need to talk to you."

"About the raids?"

"Yes. We've heard that Paiutes are killing some who cross their lands. Is that true?"

Numaga's lips twisted down at the corners and his nostrils flared. "There are many who deserve death. Every day messages come from my people telling me about the white man's outrages on our land. Yet, we still hope for peace. I speak for all my people. No blood have we taken."

"Then . . ."

"The Pitt River, Gosh-Utes, and Shoshones are angry. I do not speak for them. Only Paiutes. But I tell you this, Bolivar Roberts; my people starved through this winter. Many died."

"I was afraid of that," Bolivar whispered. "It's been a hard winter, and maybe it's not over yet. But, if you leave our relay stations in peace, we will give you food. That is my promise. I will see that no station on this line refuses any of your tribe who come in hunger."

"More promises. I am sick of promises!"

Darby's heart almost jerked up into his mouth. The chief was a hair's breadth away from violence. Violence that would leave them all dead in seconds. The desert seemed to hang in silence.

"It's not just a promise," Finney blurted. "We still have a few sacks of flour, some salt pork, and beans. Take them. Take them with our deepest appreciation."

"How will I carry these things to feed the empty bellies in my camp?"

"We give you a wagon and team. Load everything in and it's yours."

Numaga allowed himself a smile. He glanced back at Roberts. "Okay? We are not thieves."

"Of course, chief. Compliments of the Pony Express."

"And you, boss. Is it okay with you?" Bolivar asked.

"Yes, by all means."

"Good. Now neither of you can say the other was wrong." Numaga frowned. "What is this Pony Express?"

"It's a great race, chief. The mail will be relayed all the way from St. Joseph, Missouri, to San Francisco. We'll have riders going day and night, trying to breach this country in just ten days."

"Across our lands. Already I have received the stories of your camps." Numaga's eyes threw sparks. "Did you not think it wise to speak to me first?"

Darby could hear his own heart beat as the seconds thumped by.

"Chief," Finney interrupted, "it's my fault. But our route does not go through your sacred grounds near Pyramid Lake. So, we thought that . . ."

"No more!" Namaga spat. "You are like all the others who come. They poison our streams, hunt our game, and worse, they cut and burn our pinion trees for their campfires."

"That won't happen this time." Bolivar's voice was a desperate plea. "Our men are few. They do not seek gold or silver. And I'll order them not to cut the pinions which your people harvest. In return for crossing Paiute territory, we will be generous when your people are hungry."

Numaga turned and began to speak his own language to the warriors. There was no comment, but it appeared to Darby that they weren't at all pleased. Twice, the chief made rapid motions indicating food and that seemed to win grudging acceptance.

"It will begin as you ask," Numaga said, turning back to them. "I trust you, Bolivar Roberts, and I have told the others you have sworn to cross our lands in peace. You will not cut our trees, nor empty yourselves in our waterholes, as is the white man's way. And always, you will feed our hungry. If this is done, you have nothing to fear. If it is not, your camps will disappear like sand in a desert wind."

Both Finney and Roberts were nodding vigorously, and Darby was surprised to find himself doing the same. They knew this was no idle threat; one word and Chief Numaga could unleash a war that could sweep a bloody trail clear to Salt Lake City.

"You will see," Bolivar grated. "The Pony Express will be a friend to all Paiutes."

Numaga said nothing. His eyes penetrated each of them and finally he said, "There are many who council war around our campfires. But they have not seen the great numbers of whites across the Sierras. I, alone, have seen. I am leader of the Paiutes just as my father, Winnemucca, was before."

"He was a great man, Numaga," Bolivar said. "He kept the peace and your tribe grows."

"Perhaps. But now, the whites flock to Sun Mountain for gold and silver. The peace between the red and the white man is being chopped away like our trees. Keep your word, Bolivar Roberts. We will not starve as old men, hugging our naked ribs. Better to die as warriors in battle!"

With that, he reined away and slowly rode up onto the barren hillside to watch the provisions being loaded for his people.

"I'm afraid," Finney said after a time, "we'll have to go back to Carson City for additional supplies."

Bolivar nodded. "Keeping our promise and the bellies of his people full will be the best money that Russell, Majors, and Waddell ever spent."

Darby nodded in agreement. This was his first experience with Indians and it was one he'd never forget.

"Where did he . . ."

"Learn his English?" Bolivar asked.

"Yes."

"He was sent to California to be educated in a missionary school. Numaga is a very intelligent and well-

educated man. He's smart enough to know our
strengths, and our weaknesses. That makes him ten
times more dangerous as an enemy. God help the Pony
Express and the people of this territory if anything
goes wrong."

"It won't," Finney said abruptly. "I'll see that every
man on our western line understands our pledge. We
can't be responsible for immigrants, but I'll be damned
if the Pony Express doesn't do everything humanly
possible to keep the peace. Now, let's get back to Carson City."

Darby sat down at the desk and began to work on
his notes.

It is very cold today, the last before the momentous
occasion. Less than a week ago, the final decision was
made and young Warren Upson was chosen as the best
man to handle the Sierra crossing. But now, I confess I
am worried. Telegraph communication, which ends here
in Carson City, reports a blizzard raging up above. The
Marysville Stage, which has not missed a schedule in three
years, is stopped. All coaches westbound for California
are trapped at Strawberry Valley. It appears the mountain
passes are now impassable. But, tomorrow, April 3, 1860,
a lone rider, barely more than a youth, must meet the test.

We have asked ourselves if everything possible has been
done so that this event will be successful. In my opinion,
it has. But no one counted on the cruelty of nature in
striking us with a blizzard this late in the year.

This very morning, Bolivar Roberts has decided to try to
scale the Sierras with a team of pack mules in the desperate hope of beating a trail through the deepest snows.
All is ready and, as I was partly responsible for the choice
of young Upson, I must go too. The hour is at hand.

> D. Buckingham
> Alias, The Derby Man

Warren Upson's stomach was churning, and the
wind-driven snow plastered his clothes. It was early
yet, only 7:30, but how he wanted to leave. Back and
forth, he paced outside the station at Sportsman's Hall,
halfway up the western side of the Sierras. Eighty-five

miles to the east lay Carson City. In this weather, it would be the longest ride of his life.

"Come on," he whispered, "give me a few extra minutes, Bill Hamilton, or I'll never meet the schedule."

But making the schedule *was* going to be impossible. That wasn't what set him to pacing anxiously. East of Carson City, there were fellas like Bob Haslam who'd have good hard terrain over which to run. One way or another, those men would make up the time lost, minute by precious minute, all the way to St. Joseph. What scared Upson was the possibility that he might fail completely, perhaps become mired down in a snowdrift. The Sierras could do that—and worse. It could harden the blood in his veins and kill with its numbing wrath. He wasn't afraid of freezing to death; he'd even heard it was painless. But not this time, not today, when he'd be a part of this historic first-crossing. He was riding for glory—for a place in Darby Buckingham's book and others that would no doubt follow. He had to make it.

Up above, all was a howling whiteness. The wind shrieked its warning and Upson shook his head in exasperation. He'd begged Bolivar Roberts for this stretch and even Mr. Buckingham had supported him. Somehow, some way, he had to make it. Upson pushed the thought from his mind and, as he had a dozen times in the past three hours, he went to examine his mount. He'd passed over the two other animals who were faster in preference for the stocky, trail-wise bay. During the previous week, he'd had idle time to gauge the speed and endurance of each horse. Yes, the bay was a trifle slower, but it was also the most powerful animal, and as sure-footed as a mountain goat. It would have to be. They'd be breaking a fresh trail through the Sierra passes. One missed step and . . .

Warren heard the cry. "Hamilton is coming! I heard him sound his horn."

He whipped around to the station tender. "Are you sure? It's half an hour early."

As if in answer, out of the whiteness loomed the rider. His mount was faltering badly when he reached the station, but off came the mochila. It had slits for the saddlehorn and the cantle, and they had it on the bay in less than thirty seconds. Then Upson swung into the saddle.

"How can you make it?" Bill Hamilton shouted between his cupped hands as the wind beat his voice away.

"I will," he cried. "See you on the way back!"

Then, he was racing into the blinding whiteness, feeling the icy gale drive right through his coat and heavy woolen underwear. But he didn't think about that. The snow wasn't deep, only a few inches at this elevation. Now, now was the time to make speed. In another few hours, he'd be thousands of feet higher. That would be the real test of horse and man.

On he went, changing horses at stations as the snow grew thicker, colder, more determined to bury him and the world across which he passed in shrouded silence. He bent low in the saddle, trying to see into the maelstrom that buffeted him from every direction. Speed became impossible and, more and more, he found himself urging his horse through drifts. Don't get lost, don't get lost, he told himself over and over. He thought he was, until he found the Strawberry Station; they had to lift him out of the saddle.

"You can't go on," the stationmaster said flatly.

Upson's teeth were chattering, but there was no hesitation in his words. "You can't stop me and neither can this mountain!"

"The passes are closed."

"Then I'll make my own," he gritted. "Change that mochila, your two minutes are up."

Upson tipped forward in his saddle and struggled to recognize the landmarks he knew so well: here, a large fallen tree; there, a mound of rocks. He could barely see. The pass up ahead acted like a funnel and the blizzard roared straight into his face. Normally, this was a well-traveled road, heavily freighted with Comstock supplies going east and ore coming west. But not this day. Nothing moved. Only wind and whiteness.

He dismounted frequently to claw at the snow,

hunting for wagon ruts. All about him were deep
gorges, heavy with frozen streams. In some places, he
rounded the side of a mountain where the dropoff was
a thousand feet. One misstep and . . .

His pony was exhausted. As it tackled one drift after
another, Upson could hear its grunts as it tried to buck
its way through. He tumbled out of the saddle and began to pull on the reins. "Come *on!*" he shouted.

The solid feel of dry ground pulled him out of his
stupor. They'd circled a mountain and the wind
shivered off the ridges like a ghostly cape flapping
madly. Here, the snow was lighter and Upson mounted
and urged his horse into a trot. They went almost a
mile before the horse braced in its tracks. He slashed it
with his quirt. "Don't quit on me now," he pleaded.
The animal's sweat was frozen; its ears pricked forward. No amount of urging could make it budge. Upson dismounted, fumbled at the reins and yanked with
all his strength.

All at once, the very air grew still, then quivered,
and the ground shook with a deep whisper. A thousand
tons and more of white mass launched down the mountain. It started slowly, gathered momentum, and then
plunged majestically down over the trail ahead until
everything in his sight was obliterated. Upson stood
rooted, feeling the earth roll and his heart squeezing
and pounding inside. Later, when the air cleared and
he could see, what had been a ravine below was gone.

He took a deep breath and expelled it in a cloud of
vapor. If they'd gone another forty yards, their bodies
wouldn't have been discovered until July. No rider, no
mail, no fame. He gave his horse a quick pat on the
neck.

He studied the fresh, resting snow and the pass
ahead that he must reach. The trail had vanished. He
had to find another way and he'd better do it quick.
How far to the next station? Six or seven miles? If only
he could make it, there would be a fresh horse and the
summit could be breasted. But, between him and Friday's Station lay the pass. And now, he wasn't even
sure how to get that far. His spirits sagged; his body
was numb and unresponsive. All he wanted to do was

to sit and rest for a few minutes. He felt sleepy. Perhaps, a small rest, then he could . . .

"What's the matter with you, Warren Upson!" he shouted. "You want to die? Go ahead and rest!"

Angrily, he drove himself up the hillside on foot. His lungs burned in the thin air, but he kept moving until, at last, he had a clear view of the pass ahead. For almost a full minute, he stood braced against the wind. He *had* to be sure every detail of the land was remembered during the next few hours—where the drifts were deepest, where avalanches lay in wait. Satisfied, he sledded all the way down to the pony.

It took him three agonizing hours to reach the final pass over the mountains, beyond which lay Friday's Station. During that time, he never once climbed into the saddle. To do so would have killed the horse and heightened his own chances of freezing. So he walked and crawled and battled on through the snow.

Darby saw him first, though it was a long time before he was sure. For five hours, they'd been dragging the line of mules back and forth through the pass. Whipping, cajoling, pleading and, when all else failed, throwing their own bodies down in the drifts to make headway. And they'd made it!

Chilled to the bone, sheeted with ice, they'd broken through and then gone back and forth to keep it open. Darby had just returned to the western opening. He was preparing to go back through when he saw the figure emerge.

"Upson," he bellowed. "Upson!"

Like a bull, he charged through the chest-high drifts to reach the young rider. He bent down and pulled Upson erect.

"You made it, boy. You made it!"

The rider nodded weakly. Somehow, he grinned. "I guess we did," he rattled. "Help me stand and let's get this over with. I must be *hours* late."

Tears rolled down Darby's cheeks, only to freeze in seconds. He gently lifted the rider up and half-carried him those last few yards to the beaten path.

"Can you go any further?"

Warren Upson's eyes followed the cleared trail through the pass. "Is that Mr. Roberts up ahead?"

"Yes, he and a couple of others who volunteered to act as a welcoming committee."

"My, oh my," Upson said huskily, "never did any man have a better one. Help me into the saddle, Mr. Buckingham. The hard part is over."

Darby did more than help him up. He placed him on the horse as easily as he might have a child. "See you in Carson City, Mr. Upson."

The young man grinned stiffly. "U-P-S-O-N, don't spell it wrong now."

"Not a chance," Darby laughed as he watched him ride away. "Not a chance."

On April 12, Darby Buckingham was pacing back and forth in front of the tiny Pony Express Office. On the main street of Carson City dozens of townsfolk were doing likewise. They kept glancing east, and the same question was in every mind—would the Pony Express rider arrive in time?

Eight days had passed since Warren Upson handed over the mail to Pony Bob Haslam. Everyone knew the schedule: Haslam would race on to Churchill where H. J. Faust would take it to Ruby Valley, followed by Josh Perkins to Shell Creek, and then Jim Gentry's route clear to Deep Creek. After that came "Let" Huntington and John Fisher, followed by Major Egan into Salt Lake City.

Across the entire West, the timetables were laid out with precision; eight hours by steamer from San Francisco to Sacramento; from Sacramento to Carson City, fourteen hours in good weather; Carson to Salt Lake City, ninety-four hours; Salt Lake to St. Joseph, one hundred twenty-four hours. All together, two hundred forty hours. Yet, because of the Sierra blizzard, they'd gotten off to a poor start. But no one was blaming Warren Upson. In fact, he was a hero.

Now, everyone was waiting for the mail from the East. Their question could be answered only by the incoming rider.

Bolivar Roberts kept dragging out his pocket watch

and Darby was chewing the ends off his Cuban cigars.

"It's almost half past three," Bolivar fretted. "If Pony Bob doesn't get here soon, there's no way we can get the mail to San Francisco on schedule."

"Young Upson can shave time," Darby replied. "The weather has been clear ever since he passed through."

"It'll be worse on his return to California."

"Worse! How . . ."

"The run-off," Bolivar interrupted. "Those passes will be a gutter of mud clogged with stranded Washoe freight wagons. And down in the gorges there will be swollen rivers where there isn't supposed to be anything but dry creek beds."

"He'll still make it," Darby swore. "Where in blazes is that rider?"

Bolivar ordered two of his friends up on the rooftop, and together he and Darby hurried over to the waiting rider.

"Are you all set?" Darby asked.

"Sure," Upson said. "Mr. Roberts, don't you worry. At Friday's Station, we have a pony with hooves like a duck. We'll fly over that mud."

"I hope it also has fins, boy. You may have to swim. You can, can't you?" Bolivar asked with sudden concern.

The rider laughed. "I can swim, but I won't have to. I know every creek and wash from here to Sacramento. I've been going over each step of the way for days and . . ."

"Rider coming. It's . . . it's him!" The lookouts began jumping up and down on the roof. In his excitement, one of them slipped and came rolling down to crash into the street. But no one noticed; every man, woman, and child in Carson City, along with half the population of the Comstock Lode, was charging out toward the prairie.

"Give him room," Bolivar cried. "Oh hell. Upson, go out and change on the flats before these folks cause a stampede."

"Yes, sir!"

Darby was so excited he grabbed a horse and

mounted without needing to climb up on something first. Several other men were firing off their guns and people were cheering so loudly that Pony Bob, though still at least two miles out, began to wave his hat. It must have been a frightening sight to the exhausted rider. More like rushing into a cavalry charge than a welcoming crowd.

Upson easily outdistanced the mob. His pony was so fast it made Darby think his own borrowed steed was part mule. He saw Upson meet the oncoming rider, and then both men were on the ground running. It was a lightning change and, before anyone could quite believe his eyes, Pony Bob was standing alone watching a cloud of dust recede toward the next station at Genoa. Darby reined his horse to a walk.

"What time is it?" Haslam panted.

"Three thirty-one."

"Damn. I'm a full minute late. Bolivar's going to give me hell."

"No, he isn't. My watch always runs fast. You're undoubtedly a few minutes early."

"Well, hooray!"

The saloons were busy that evening and both Darby and Bolivar drank stupendous quantities of whiskey. They each lamented the fact that they couldn't be in Sacramento and San Francisco where California's biggest celebrations ever were being planned. Flags would line the streets, cannons would boom, and bands would play. Yet, none of those things mattered—the Pony Express worked. Now, all that remained was to see if it could somehow meet the 240-hour schedule.

TELEGRAM:

APRIL 13, 1860

5:25 P.M.

BOLIVAR:

WE MADE IT IN 239 HOURS STOP GREAT CELEBRATIONS STOP CITY GOING WILD STOP CONGRATULATIONS.

WM. FINNEY
SAN FRANCISCO, CALIFORNIA

Chapter 4

Howard Clayton gazed out the doorway of his ranch house toward the Sierras. It was early morning, and the old man felt crotchety and stiff as he always did before the sun warmed his joints. To the west, between his own spread and the mountains, was Carson Valley. Lush and green, it was good cattle country but already claimed, first by the Mormons, then later, when they'd been called back to Salt Lake City, by a swarm of new-comers.

He could have had a pretty sizeable ranch if he'd been interested enough to file for water rights and make the improvements. Hell, he could even have staked a few of Genoa's city lots. There was good profit in fleecing the hordes of Washoe-bound miners. But he hadn't cared enough to go after it. As far as Clayton was concerned, the Nevada Territory was a barren, God-forsaken wilderness. If it weren't for the gold and silver they were discovering up on the Com-stock, nobody except the Indians would live here. And the fortunes attracted only men who were illiterate scum from around the world.

Clayton spat tobacco juice and grimaced. That was another uncivilized habit he'd acquired. When he re-turned to Virginia, took back his land and rightful place among gentlemen, he'd resume smoking the long, rich cigars he favored. But right now, he just didn't have the money, and the cigars out in this country were awful.

How much longer would it be until he returned to the South? Clayton believed the answer depended on how effectively he crippled the Pony Express. Until now, not one of his letters to the men who were preparing to uphold the glorious Southern tradition had been answered. They were shunning him, goddamn their righteous hides! Well, that would all change when he, Howard Horatio Clayton, stopped the Pony Express. Then they'd beg him to come back to Virginia. Yes, and give him an office in the Confederacy.

The thought made him smile. While Jefferson Davis and all the other big talkers debated endlessly about secession, he would be *doing something*—the first step was going to be his and it would make him a hero.

"Hey, boss."

Clayton turned and saw Tulley. The man was knuckling sleep from his eyes and trying to button his shirt at the same time. Once again, Clayton was taken by the very enormity he witnessed. Tulley scared him sometimes. In addition to his huge proportions, there was a definite cruel streak.

"Yeah?" Clayton answered.

"I was in Genoa yesterday. They're expecting another rider to come through. That'll make the fourth. How long are we going to wait?"

"Until I figure out a way to block them," Clayton swore impatiently.

"Hell, if we don't do somethin' pretty quick, the Indians are gonna do it for us. Then, we won't get nothin' from Jefferson Davis like you been sayin'."

"What about the Indians?" Clayton asked, his interest sharpening. "Have you heard anything new?"

"It's going around they've been raiding some."

"Who?" Clayton snapped. "Numaga?"

"Naw. I heard he's fasting, trying to keep the Paiutes from doing any killing. Seems all the trouble right now is with the Pitts and Gosh-Utes."

That was too bad. Damn that Numaga. Only the Paiutes were strong enough to put the Pony out of business.

Clayton scowled. "If we could get Numaga riled up, he'd *have* to start raiding."

"You can rile him up if you want," Tulley said with his beefy face dead serious, "but I don't want no part of those Indians. I've seen the way they can shoot arrows."

Clayton looked up quickly. "A couple of weeks ago, you had some. I watched you practicing."

"Still got 'em, but I cracked the damn bow."

"How many arrows do you have left?" Clayton felt his blood begin to quicken.

"Three or four, but . . ." his voice squeezed off and the confusion in his eyes changed to a shrewd gleam. "Boss, I know what you're thinking."

For the first time in weeks, Clayton laughed. "When it comes down to it, Tulley, you're a hell of a lot smarter than you look."

The huge man grinned wolfishly. "You bet I am. And you'd do well to remember it, Mr. Clayton. I'll get the boys and the arrows."

He stopped. "We're riding this morning, ain't we?"

Clayton saw the eagerness and, for some reason, the old man shivered with the thought that Tulley would go ahead without him rather than wait. "Yeah," he said, "we ride now."

Tulley slammed his immense paws together in obvious delight. "I sure wish I hadn't cracked that bow."

"You can put the arrows in without it."

"Sure I can. Right down the bullet holes."

Clayton nodded, uncertain he could bury the revulsion he felt. When word got back to Carson City, all hell would break loose. The townspeople and every able-bodied miner on the Comstock would be calling for Paiute blood. They'd attack Numaga and the fighting would grow. Maybe someday they'd call it the Pony Express War. They might as well. With six thousand Paiutes, the Pitts, Shoshones, Bannocks, and other scattered tribes, it would take years before the dust settled and things got peaceable. By then, the Pony Express would have ceased to exist—just like the Union.

It was late afternoon, and hot for being so early in the spring. All morning, Clayton and his men had followed the Carson River east. They'd ridden close to the water, under the big cottonwoods where they wouldn't be spotted. Dayton was the first Pony Express station, and they'd made a wide detour and continued on. Tulley and Clayton agreed they'd wait until they reached an almost empty station not likely to be visited by miners.

"There's Churchill," Tulley said, pointing down at the adobe building.

"Let's give it a look-see." Clayton nudged his horse down a hillside toward the station. He saw two men. It looked right.

"Hold up, Mr. Clayton. Don't you come any closer."

"Damn," Tulley swore softly. "The other one jumped inside."

He'd done more than just go inside. Clayton saw a rifle barrel poke meanly at them from a gunport in the wall.

"What do you want?" the hostler yelled.

"Got any food?"

"Not for you. I'm on the Pony Express payroll and I was in Carson when you and that big one tried to kill Mr. Roberts and Mr. Buckingham." He waved the gun. "Any closer and we start shootin'."

"He means it, boss," one of the riders said nervously.

"Shut up," Tulley hissed, twisting sideways. "We can still take them."

"No," Clayton sighed. "There's no reason. We'll just keep riding until we come to a station where they've never seen me. Then, it will be quick and easy."

Tulley nodded. He didn't look very happy, but Clayton figured the hell with it. One Pony Express station was as good as another. No sense in taking chances.

"That's it, Williams Station." Clayton glanced back at the narrow canyon through which their horses had just had to swim. He was tired and wet and sick of staying off the trail. It was late afternoon and he'd gone far enough for one day. His bones were chilled and aching.

"Hello," he called, motioning his riders forward along the gravelled riverbed.

Two men stepped out of a wooden shack. It had a rock fireplace and a corral in the rear and sat about a hundred yards above the water. Smoke curled lazily up to the cloudless sky, and he could smell pork frying.

"Howdy, strangers. Come on in. Supper's in the pan."

Tulley grinned at all of them and whispered, "I'll do the shooting. Ain't got enough arrows to plug a mess of bullet holes."

As they rode up toward the station, Clayton scanned the hillsides, looking for anyone who might be watching. Nothing moved. There were no sounds of either pick or shovel, only the deep gurgling of the water below where the canyon pinched into rapids.

"It's all clear, Tulley. Make each shot count."

The giant spurred his horse a half-stride into the lead. Clayton saw the big teeth exposed in what was supposed to pass as a grin. It looked more like a death grimace.

The hostler cupped his hands over his eyes and squinted into the dying sun. "You fellas riding in from . . . hey!"

Tulley's bullet caught him right through the left shirt pocket and the hostler spun around in a crazy dance, his face draining as he tripped and fell. The second employee didn't fare any better. He'd pivoted and tried to get back inside. Tulley shot him in the back and he arched at the waist, then grabbed the door frame with both hands. He didn't try to turn, he only stood there on his toes with that arching spine. Tulley's second bullet drove in between the shoulder blades and knocked him down as if he'd been pole-axed.

"Pretty good shootin', huh, boss?" Tulley asked, turning his gun back and forth in admiration.

Clayton nodded and looked at the others. Their lips were pursed in a tight line and both men seemed a little unnerved.

Clayton nodded with a short, jerking motion. "You did well. It was fine shooting."

The giant laughed outright. "Did you see the look on that first one's face? Man, was he . . ."

Clayton's mouth twisted in disgust. "Forget how he looked. Tulley, bring along the arrows. I want to get this over with."

The laughter faded; he turned slack and then angry.
"What's the matter?" he stormed. "I did the dirty
work! You oughta be grateful."

"We are," Clayton whispered, "but did you have to
enjoy it so much?"

"Oh, hell. I could have plugged the first one in the
stomach. But I did it clean and quick."

Clayton shook his head. "Never mind. Forget I said
anything. Just poke the arrows in them and drag 'em
somewhere out back."

Tulley nodded, motioning for the others to dismount
and help. "Let's hurry. I can almost taste that meat
cookin'."

The older man swallowed noisily. He wasn't hungry
anymore. Just cold.

By the time they'd dragged the station tenders
around the shack and covered them with horse blankets, the meat was burned. Smoke filled the cabin and
they'd been obliged to cook more pork, after waving
blankets around to clear the air. Maybe that's what
brought the four Paiutes in from the desert hills. At
least, that was how Clayton figured it.

Now, as they sat their horses out in the station yard
and motioned first to their stomachs, then to their
mouths, it was plain they expected to be fed.

Clayton and Tulley went out to try to get rid of
them while the others stayed inside with leveled rifles.

"I can make 'em go away, boss."

"Leave your gun be."

"They ain't listening to you, damnit. We can't have
Indians snooping around with them two fellas laid out
cold behind the station!" Tulley clucked his tongue
softly. "But I wouldn't mind entertaining those two
squaws these fellas got. Didn't know they had such
pretty women."

Clayton ignored the remark. His mind was racing
again. He'd noticed the squaws, too. At first, he'd felt
only relief that there were just two braves armed with
just bows and arrows. No threat. They were merely an
irritation to be disposed of.

But now, a new idea was forming. He stared at the

squaws. Very young, both of them. And Tulley was right—they were *damned* good-looking.

"Why don't we invite them in for supper?" he heard himself say.

"Why not just invite the squaws in?" Tulley asked. "I'm sure the boys won't mind."

"Hmmm. Maybe that's not such a bad idea."

"You mean it, boss?"

Clayton turned his head sideways. Tulley's eyes were bright and he was already flushed. "If you want them squaws, I'm sure not going to get in your way. But their braves might have other ideas."

"We can take care of 'em," Tulley swallowed.

"Just one thing before you start. If you and the others are set to have a little fun tonight, I'm game. But I want those two braves to walk out of here alive."

"Are you crazy? Why, they'd head straight back to Numaga and . . ." Tulley's voice tapered off and a gleam of understanding flickered on his face and a slow smile formed.

"I'm always one step ahead of you, Tulley. But you catch on quick." He pivoted back to the Indians and began to nod his head.

They tied their horses to the corral and slowly walked forward, the men in front, the squaws behind.

"Get 'em in here," Tulley called.

Clayton stopped at the door and motioned them to follow. There was a hasty discussion and the Indians made it clear they wanted to eat in the yard.

"Goddamnit!" Tulley raged.

With a frozen smile, calculated to put the visitors at ease, Clayton drawled, "Bring the vittles out. Then grab 'em when they reach for the plates."

Clayton kept grinning. His expression never changed while his men brought out the food. The two braves stepped forward and held out their hands. That's when Tulley dropped his plate in the dirt and nearly decapitated one with a blow to the face that knocked him sprawling. The second Indian was quickly overpowered and beaten almost senseless.

One squaw made it halfway to the river before Tulley pulled her down. Clayton heard Tulley slap her twice and she quit kicking up the carpet of dead leaves under the trees. Clayton turned away to see the two braves staggering into the brush. Inside the cabin, a table crashed and someone laughed. The other squaw began to yell and her cries were instantly stifled.

Clayton walked up to the cabin and thought about it for a few moments. He'd never had an Indian. Maybe his men thought he was too old for that kind of thing.

They were wrong. He strode inside and slammed the door.

"Take a rifle and hike upriver about a mile," Clayton ordered. He extracted his pocket watch. "What time does that Pony Express rider reach Carson?"

"Early afternoon," Tulley replied. "Around three or three-thirty."

"Then he'll be coming through here anytime. All you have to do is ambush him. Then we'll put an arrow in him like with the others. Bolivar Roberts may be able to keep the deaths of two station tenders quiet, but he can't hide the killing of a rider or losing the mail."

Tulley scowled and looked toward the cabin. "Why don't you send one of the others? Hell, I'd rather be in there with those squaws then hidin' in the brush somewheres."

"You had more than your share last night. Besides, I don't trust them."

Tulley still didn't look convinced. Clearly, his mind was on the women. Clayton frowned, trying to decide how to handle this man. "All right," he conceded. "We'll stay on until midnight. You can have one later. But right now, we've got work to do. That rider has to be shot before he reaches this clearing or he's going to see that something is wrong."

"How soon before they know in Carson City?"

"Bolivar will be riding by sundown," Clayton mused. "He'll be here by midnight, and all they'll find is three bodies with Paiute arrows in 'em and a pile of ashes where the cabin used to be."

"It all fits, doesn't it? We've even got those Indian ponies to leave tracks around the yard."

Clayton hadn't thought of that. Somehow, it irritated him that Tulley would come up with it instead of himself. He peered at the giant until the man began to squirm.

"What are you staring at me for?"

Clayton looked away. "No reason. Look, ahh, you take care of business and I won't forget when we take our places in the South."

"You better not. It galls me to leave with them others pleasurin' themselves inside." His eyes, deep set under huge brows, narrowed. "What happens to the squaws? We gonna kill 'em?"

"Have to. Otherwise, they'd tell Numaga about us ambushing the Pony Express rider. Once he found out about that, he might decide not to attack the other stations. Those two braves are sure we work here but, by tonight, the squaws will have figured something different."

"What a waste. I don't like killin' women."

"They aren't women. They're savages."

"Maybe. But you can't tell me they didn't feel like women."

Clayton flushed deeply, remembering last night. Inside the cabin, he heard one of his men laugh and he suddenly felt a twinge of shame. Maybe they were just squaws, but . . .

"What's the matter, boss?"

"Nothing, I guess. But I just changed my mind. I'm going with you."

"Thought you trusted me."

"I do." He turned away so the man couldn't see his face. "Do me a favor. My rifle is inside. You get it. And tell the boys what's going on."

Tulley laughed. "You old devil. You ain't got enough control to come back out again, have you?"

Clayton spun around, wanting to slap the man, but fear overrode his anger. "Just get the goddamn rifle, Tulley. And let's go!"

"Sure, boss. Anything you say."

*   *   *

Because Clayton wasn't as strong, they chose a firing position only a hundred yards east of the station. Yet, they agreed it would be a good place for the ambush. The Pony Express rider, Bob Haslam, would pass less than two hundred feet away. Between them, there was no chance of missing, no chance at all. And their vantage point offered a perfect view of the station, as well as east along the trail.

Claude Tulley tried to find comfortable seating in between the rocks. But the space was cramped and he was impatient. It irritated him that the old man hadn't chosen someone else. He deserved to be rewarded more often, and he couldn't think of a better way than of spending this time with the women.

"Look!"

Tulley started and his rifle scraped along the rock. "What?"

"Two men. About a quarter of a mile downriver. They're hiding in those cottonwoods."

"I see them. What do you think they're doing?"

"They're spying on the cabin."

"Look to me like prospectors." Tulley squinted. "I never seen either one of 'em before."

Clayton swore bitterly. "Now what are we going to do? They're already suspicious or they'd have just walked up and knocked."

"Maybe, but they didn't see us leave or they'd be more cautious."

"We'll have to take care of them anyway," Clayton gritted. "They've seen our horses."

Tulley began to rise, but something moved in the corner of his vision and all at once the two prospectors flattened against a tree.

"What's going on?"

He took a deep breath and let it out slowly. "I hate to tell you this, boss, but there's a passle of Indians sneaking up from the other side. Those two we chased off last night must have found help mighty fast."

"What are we going to do about the rider?"

Tulley pulled his rifle back and cradled it against his chest. He leaned against the rock and shut his eyes. "You can do what you want, as long as it's some-

wheres else. I saw at least a dozen Paiutes moving
through those cottonwoods. So did those two prospectors. That's why they've played rabbit."

"The Indians won't see 'em. Damn the luck!"

"No," Tulley replied. "And we sure can't do anything about it."

"Our boys are as good as scalped."

"They didn't do much anyway," Tulley grumbled.
"Maybe that Bob Haslam fella will ride smack into
that hornet's nest and we won't have to fake anything."

Clayton removed his hat. The man's hair was dead
gray and petered out along the top. "Maybe it won't
come out so bad after all."

"For us, it won't. I just pity those poor bastards inside."

"They're almost to the cabin!"

"I don't want to see 'em die getting scalped." Tulley
involuntarily ran his fingers through his own thick,
black hair and he shivered. He'd once seen a man
who'd been scalped. Ever since that day, he'd been
thinking about it off and on, sometimes late at night. If
he got caught by Indians, he'd make them finish him
quick. Paiutes, he'd been told, could torture their enemies a long, long time.

"Stay down," Tulley warned. "Don't let them see
you."

"Relax. They're . . . they're rushing the cabin,"
Clayton gasped. "My God, there must be twenty of
'em."

Several moments passed and Tulley realized he was
bracing himself for the screams. "What are they doing?"

Clayton's voice sounded old. "They're dragging the
men outside, face first. They're . . . they're naked."

Tulley shivered.

"John and Ben are pleading. Now, they're pointing
to our horses, trying to . . ." Clayton's voice caught in
his throat. "They're on their knees!"

"They're meat," Tulley whispered. "Are they scalp-
ing 'em yet?"

"No. They've brought the two squaws out, wrapped

in blankets. Both of them are spitting on Ben and John."

Tulley clenched his hands together until his knuckles were white. "I don't want to hear any more."

"Oh . . . no!"

"What. What happened?"

Clayton sagged. "You'll have to see for yourself. I've seen enough."

Tulley waited a long time before he made himself twist around and look. He felt queasy and surprisingly weak. But he *had* to see. Maybe the squaws would tell their men about him and Clayton. Maybe they'd start hunting for tracks. And they'd find them! He and Clayton hadn't thought to brush tracks away. Maybe they were coming up now.

They weren't. The Paiutes were setting fire to the station. Already he could see gray smoke boiling out the cabin door. The bodies had to be inside. The warriors began to whoop and dance as the flames grew bolder.

Tulley watched in fascination. He saw part of the roof drop in and tongues of fire lick toward the sky. Then, the Indians gathered all the horses and faded into the trees with their two squaws.

He sagged with relief. "It's over. They took their women and left."

Clayton edged up beside him. There was a sheet of perspiration on his face that made Tulley realize he wasn't the only one who'd been afraid. Most likely, the old man's thoughts had mirrored his own. "We're damned lucky, boss. The way that fire is going, there won't be any signs left that we've been here."

"Yeah. I guess you're right," Clayton said quietly. "There's nothing that could . . . wait a minute!"

"What's wrong now?"

"The prospectors. Do you see them?"

Tulley swung his attention back to the cottonwoods. "They're gone!"

"We've got to find them. They were close enough to hear the pleading."

"So what?"

"So they probably heard Ben and John telling those Indians that *we* were the ones needed killing."

"You can't be sure," Tulley said doggedly. "We couldn't hear what they were saying."

"You want to take the chance? I saw those boys pointing toward the horses. You figure it out."

Tulley swore. Clayton was right. The prospectors would have counted six horses and only four men, any one of whom they might have recognized as being on Clayton's payroll. So it really didn't matter what they'd heard before Ben and John were killed. Hell, it was even possible they'd been spying since yesterday when they'd grabbed the squaws.

"All right," he said bitterly, "what do you want to do, wait until Haslam rides in and kill him first?"

"Hell, no," Clayton snapped. "That's unnecessary now. This makes it cleaner. The only thing left to tie us in are those prospectors. We've *got* to find them."

"Easier said than done. These hills are crawling with their kind."

"You'd recognize them, wouldn't you?"

The old man was staring at him. Tulley tried to remember those faces. But they'd been in shadow, a quarter of a mile away. "Would you?"

Clayton's mouth drew down at the corners and his voice came out waspish. "You're younger than me. My eyes aren't as sharp as they were at your age. I was counting on you!"

"I don't know, boss." He scrubbed his face tiredly. "Maybe I could. But I'm not sure."

"You better be. Our necks might just depend on it."

Tulley started to rise. "I'll try. They both had beards, didn't they?"

Clayton's expression was filled with contempt. "I think so. But that sure isn't going to narrow it any. Most every prospector in the territory has a beard. Sit down."

"Why?" The old man was really starting to nettle him. Tulley watched the last of the roof timbers crash in and saw the flames squeeze up higher. He needed a drink and time to think about everything. He fancied he could smell burnt hair and that made his stomach churn all over again.

"We're staying put until Haslam rides through. The thing we *don't* need is to have him see us."

Tulley eased back and closed his eyes. "Why don't you tell me about Virginia again?" he asked hopefully. "You know, the part about those big plantations and those Southern belles that have waists so small I could wrap my two hands around their middles."

But Clayton said nothing. Maybe he was thinking about those men in the cabin. That was a mistake. Talking about Virginia would have been better. Damn that old man anyway, Tulley thought angrily. Sometimes, I'd like to put my hands around his neck and squeeze until . . .

"He's coming," Clayton hissed.

Tulley sat up. For a moment, his eyes fixed on Clayton's red neck. It was skinney, like a chicken's, and had a big knot which moved up and down when he swallowed.

"He's reining up," Clayton giggled. "There he goes. Flogging the hell out of his pony, going straight for Carson City."

Tulley watched the rider disappear and then stood up. "Guess it's time we started walking. Them prospectors got a big lead."

"We'll find 'em," Clayton said grimly. "One way or another, we'll find 'em."

Chapter 5

Claude Tulley felt weary, and they hadn't even started the long walk back to the Carson Valley. It had taken him almost two hours to locate the prospector's camp, or at least what remained of it. Now it was nearly sundown and the two witnesses had vanished. Old man Clayton was enraged.

"Goddamnit, we've got to find them," he swore.

"We will, boss," Tulley said absently. He sauntered over to the hole in the rocks where the two miners obviously had been hoping to make their strike. Inside, he could identify picks and a rock hammer scattered on the floor. There was a pile of rocks along one side of the wall and he scooped several up for closer inspection.

"Can you tell gold if you see it, boss?"

"What do you want to know for?"

"If this tunnel shows any promise, those two fellas will come back for sure." He stepped out into the fading light and chipped at the rock with his thumbnail. "Looks to me like it's nothing but quartz."

Clayton snapped his fingers. "Say, wouldn't those fellas have this claim staked?"

"They might."

"Then let's see if we can find their stakeposts. Their names would be stuffed in a can, most likely."

Tulley nodded and strode away. He sure hoped they found something. The old man was starting to get under his skin.

"Over here," Clayton shouted.

Tulley hurried to see Clayton tear a slip of paper out of an empty bean can that had been tacked to a corner post.

"It says this claim is deeded to Rollie Evans and

Hank Brown. They've been here five weeks." Clayton scratched at the gray stubble on his face. "But, if they've headed straight for town, having their names isn't going to do much good."

"Maybe they won't tell."

"Why not?"

"Hell," Tulley said, "would you?"

"Go on, I'm listening," Clayton said, folding the paper and slipping it into his vest pocket.

"If I were those two, I'd keep my mouth shut. They were old men, boss. At least your age."

Clayton stiffened. "I'm not *that* old."

"Don't get your back up. What I'm saying is that they left here in one hell of a rush. Probably scared of those Indians coming around. They were so worried they didn't even grab their tools or . . ."

"Get to the point."

"I'm comin' to that," Tulley said hotly. "If they were *that* scared, it don't make sense they'd risk their hides by tellin' everyone about us. What do they have to gain?"

"Nothing," Clayton admitted after a long pause.

"That's right! This Evans and Brown been around too long to make a habit of sticking their necks into what don't concern 'em."

"Maybe you've got something, Tulley. These old miners are used to keeping secrets. I only wish we could be certain. Give 'em a warning or something."

Tulley strode over to the dead campfire. He knelt and retrieved a charred branch. Then, he plodded back to the cave and grabbed the pick and wrote on its handle: KEEP QUITE OR GIT SHOT.

"This ought to be clear enough," he grunted, sinking the pick into the ground. "I got me a hunch those two old fellas are somewhere up in these hills right now, watching."

"I'll tell you one thing," Clayton drawled. "For the next couple of weeks, we're going to be watching *them*. And if I so much as hear of 'em looking toward the U.S. Marshal's office, or seeing anyone employed by the Pony Express, they're buzzard bait."

It was sunset when they headed toward the Carson

River. And, right at that moment, when the sky glows, Tulley saw the two miners. Just a flash of metal among the rocks.

Tulley glanced away and kept walking. The sun was a blood-red ball on the horizon. He figured there'd been enough killing for one day. Besides, his message was damned clear.

Pony Bob Haslam fanned his pony into Carson City and passed the mochila on to Upson in silence. He nodded to Bolivar Roberts and Darby Buckingham to follow. Normally, he wore a devil-may-care grin and was quick with a joke or a laugh. But not today. Darby noticed the strain on his face and saw the young horseman's eyes were clouded with worry. They passed through the spectators and ignored the usual questions about weather, Indians, and news from the East.

"Sit down, Bob. You look used. Trouble?"

"The kind you been afraid of, Bolivar. Indians cleaned out Williams Station. Killed our hostlers. Burnt the place to the ground."

Darby rocked in his chair. "What tribe?"

"I don't know for certain. But, from the sign, I'd guess it was Paiutes."

"That's impossible!" Roberts exclaimed. "We have Numaga's word he'll keep peace."

"Then his word ain't worth spit." Haslam jerked out of his chair. "I *saw* our hostlers . . . or what was left of 'em. They had arrows stickin' out of their chests— Paiute arrows."

Bolivar's shoulders dropped and his face turned gray. "If it was the Paiutes and not some other band of renegades, we're in for a war the likes of which ain't been seen in this territory."

He strode over to a map pinned on the wall. Darby knew it well enough. There were pins for every Pony Express station between Carson City and Salt Lake.

"Look at 'em! We've got forty-one stations covering hundreds of miles across Indian territory. It's so big the army can't guarantee protection. Each station is as helpless as a pegged-down chicken in coyote country."

"There must be a reason for Numaga's actions,"

Darby mused. "We were certain he was a man of his word."

"Yeah, I was. And, for some damned reason, I still think so."

"You wouldn't if you'd seen what I did," Haslam gritted.

"But you *could* have made a mistake," Darby argued. "Perhaps those weren't Paiute arrows. Did you get off your horse and look at them closely?"

"Hell, no, Mr. Buckingham. The fire was still going. I saw the bodies and the arrows and I had my gun out, expecting those killers to charge from the trees. Their pony tracks weren't ten minutes old. Would you have stuck around to play detective?"

"Haslam," Bolivar rasped, "he was only trying to be certain."

"Never mind," Darby interrupted, "he's got a right to be angry. No, if I'd been there, I wouldn't even have slowed my horse."

"Forget what I said, Mr. Buckingham. It's just that I'm worried about my friends. All the way in, I've been wondering if those Paiutes are going after the other stations. Hell, it's like Mr. Roberts said, against a band as big as the one that hit Williams Station, our boys ain't got a chance."

"Have you told anyone what you saw?"

"No. Just the hostlers and station keepers on the way in."

"Good," Bolivar nodded. "The news will travel fast enough anyway. Someone is bound to pass through tonight or early tomorrow morning. When this town hears about it, there's going to be a riot." He grabbed his rifle and began to load. "If I ride hard, I can be back tomorrow at noon. Maybe then, I'll have a few answers or at least enough questions to stop some of the hotheads around here from going off half-cocked."

"I want to go along," Darby said. "In fact, I insist."

"I can't let you slow me down," Bolivar said flatly. "I'll be relaying Pony Express horseflesh the likes of which you've never ridden."

Darby swallowed. Racing a horse across the desert at night was about as far from his idea of having a good time as anything imaginable. Yet, he *had* to go. Up to now, he'd always prided himself on being a good judge of men. And there'd been something about Numaga that made him certain he spoke only the truth.

"I can hang on to a saddlehorn tighter than anyone you ever saw, Bolivar. You may need help and I won't slow you down."

Bolivar smiled thinly. "Don't say I didn't warn you, Darby. Okay, let's ride."

"You need one more?" Haslam asked wearily.

"No, Bob. You're tired and there aren't enough fresh horses. Rest up for the next ride. We still got a schedule to keep."

As they bulled out the door, Haslam said something that echoed Darby's own thoughts. "I *could* be wrong. Maybe they ain't Paiute arrows. Man, I sure hope I was wrong."

Between his own body weight and the standard riding saddle, the running horse he mounted was carrying an extra 140 pounds. Yet, when Darby touched heels to the animal's flanks, it bolted so fast he almost went over backward. He would have if he hadn't had a death lock on the saddlehorn. As it was, he practically ripped it off.

Then, they were galloping out of Carson City, running so hard and free that the wind's force made Darby's eyes water and his derby hat sail away in the night. He couldn't believe a horse could move like this. Outside of leaping off a cliff, no man had ever traveled at such speed.

Darby made no attempt to rein the animal and, fortunately, it seemed to have the eyes of a cat as they swept east.

Though it was late at night when they galloped into Dayton and the relays beyond, Bolivar's station men weren't asleep. In fact, at Churchill, Darby had a few bad moments when the stock tender opened up on them, thinking it was an Indian attack. They were fortunate that the man could only hear hoofbeats and his shots were off target.

The station employees were nervous, expecting the

worst, and Darby couldn't blame them. As they traded horses, there were few questions, and not one mentioned quitting or even asked for help. Each had a job to do, and they'd understood the risks when they'd signed on and taken the oath of loyalty.

Darby lost track of the hours. The rolling thunder of hoofbeats stretched on forever. The soreness he felt on his backside became a body-wide ache. He tried to relax in the saddle but, each time, his racing Pony would launch itself over brush or rock and he would nearly fall. The only solace he gained was that, now, he fully appreciated what a Pony Express rider had to endure. And they did this for only fifty dollars a month! His admiration for Warren Upson, Pony Bob Haslam, and the rest grew to boundless proportions.

His horse crashed into the one being ridden by Bolivar Roberts, and Darby instinctively yanked its head up, saving them from a grievous spill.

"Rein in, Buckingham. We're almost there," came a whisper.

Darby could have cried with joy. Even the horse, badly winded after more than twenty miles of packing such a load, seemed ready to quit.

"We're going to lead our horses the rest of the way. Williams Station is just up ahead. They may be waiting."

Darby nodded, barely managing to drag his battered leg over the cantle. When he touched the ground, he wanted to fling himself down and kiss it. His short legs felt as if they'd been poured full of sand. They were as numb as posts and three times as inflexible. The horse was standing spraddle-legged with its head down, simply fighting for air. It looked as beaten as he felt.

"Follow me. We'll stick to the trees. It'll be daybreak in the next few minutes."

"I hadn't noticed," Darby said drily. "How can you tell?"

"See that skyline to the east? You can just begin to see the gray light over the hills."

What hills? What skyline? Where was east? Darby couldn't see anything. It was pitch black down near the river and the only reason he knew they were on the Carson was the sound of water.

"Yeah," Darby sighed, not wanting Bolivar to know how useless he was at this moment.

"Follow me."

Then, before Darby could reply, Bolivar vanished. Darby snapped up, alert. He surely didn't want to be left behind. He tried to listen to the soft hoof-fall of Bolivar's mount, but his own horse was still gasping so loudly it was impossible.

To the right, Darby thought. He felt until he had the reins in his hand and then started forward. He got only a dozen or so steps before he walked, fully upright, into a cottonwood tree.

The tree staggered him, almost flattened him cold. "Blast! Blast!" Darby raged in pain.

"Shhh." The sound was close. "For God's sake, Buckingham. We're supposed to be sneaking up on the place."

Darby took his nose and gently pushed it back and forth. "Blast!" he muttered. "Broken again."

"Huh? What did you say?"

He sat down by the tree, deciding he'd gone far enough. Riding like a maniac in the dark had been punishment, yet he'd asked for it and wouldn't complain. But he'd be damned if he was going to render himself senseless trying to navigate through a forest of cottonwoods in this blackness.

"I'm waiting until I can see," he growled. "If there are Indians up ahead, I'd rather take an arrow than be bludgeoned to death by a tree trunk."

Surprisingly, Bolivar Roberts chuckled. "Yeah, it is sorta like wandering around in a bear cave." Leaves crunched as he eased down to wait. "How do you feel?"

"You don't want to know," Darby said. He tested the nose again, trying to remember how often it had been busted during his prize-fighting days—at least four or five.

"Have you come up with any new theories about why Numaga let this happen?" Bolivar whispered.

"No."

"Neither have I." He expelled a deep breath. "Well, in another hour, maybe we'll have some answers. If we don't, there's nothing that's going to stop a party from going up to fight Numaga. They'll say that the Paiutes would grow bold and start attacking everyone."

"Do you agree?"

"I don't know anymore. If Numaga has turned renegade. . ." He didn't finish. The answer was clear enough to Darby.

When there was enough light to see the mound of ashes ahead, Darby and Bolivar approached the clearing with their rifles up and ready. And, though the morning was cool down beside the river, Darby could feel the sweat popping out beneath his shirt.

He could taste the acrid smoke. It hung about the clearing like an invisible presence. He could smell something else, too. It was death.

"Over there," Roberts choked.

He nodded and kept his Winchester pointed, moving in a slow half circle as they crept forward. Ahead, he could see the pile of smoldering rubble and the bodies. They were lying on their stomachs and were badly charred. And out of them poked the burnt but clearly recognizable arrows.

Bolivar studied them, his eyes old and sick. "Paiutes," he groaned. "They're Paiute for sure."

They stared at the dead fire. Suddenly, Darby stiffened. He scrubbed his eyes and blinked. "I'm afraid," he said quietly, "those two weren't the only ones who died. Look underneath those charred beams."

Bolivar leaned down and it was a long time before he straightened. When he did, he seemed smaller. "I think there's more than one, Darby. We'd better sift through these ashes. Looks to me like we're in for a long day."

They were covered with ash, black with soot, and red-eyed from coughing. The bottoms of Darby's trousers were singed—proof that the fire hadn't been completely extinguished. They'd buried the remains of four men—two employees of the Pony Express, and a pair of strangers.

"I wonder who they were, Darby."

"Perhaps if we knew, it might answer a lot of our questions."

"What do you mean?"

Darby reached into his coat pocket. "I was thinking about these," he said.

"What are they?"

"Beads, shells, and a few pieces of ornamental silver." He glanced up. "I think they were necklaces."

"You mean jewelry?"

"Indian jewelry. There are more shells inside, but it didn't seem worthwhile to collect them all."

"What are you getting at?" Bolivar asked, leaning forward with anticipation.

"Nothing. But I'm a writer and my imagination is quite refined. I was thinking there might be a real story to this."

Bolivar's jaw tightened. "Darby, if you are fixing to invent some wild tale about my men having Indian squaws, you'd better think again."

"You misjudge my intentions," Darby soothed. "Yet, how do you explain the jewelry?"

"I can't. But we didn't find any women, and that's what's important."

"Precisely," Darby replied. "Bolivar, what time do you estimate the Paiutes raided this station?"

"Late afternoon, maybe evening. Why?"

Darby poured the charred shells from one hand to the other. He knew where his own mind was leading him. If he were correct, there *was* hope for averting an all-out war. Yet, he was reluctant to put his theory into words. Better, he thought, to drop clues one by one and see if Bolivar Roberts reached the same answer.

"You'd have to guess the hostlers would have been getting supper ready about that time," Darby mused. "And they were probably up and waiting for Pony Bob. Does that seem reasonable?"

"Sure," Bolivar said, frowning. "What are you driving at, Buckingham? Don't play word games or riddles. I'm in no mood."

"Of course not. It's apparent you're also too upset

about these deaths to notice things you might otherwise have thought strange."

"If you're still going on about those shells, they don't tell me anything. Maybe one of the visitors was peddling the damned stuff. Some do. Blankets, trinkets, baskets, all kinds of things."

"And you think that explains it?" He couldn't quite manage to keep the skepticism out of his tone.

"As well as anything. I'm telling you that some white men fancy squaw-made jewelry."

Bolivar was angry; yet, Darby knew the anger was born of worry and probably a deep-seated guilt about the loss of his employees.

"I think," Darby said, his words coming precise and measured, "some men perhaps 'fancied' the squaws themselves."

"What!" Bolivar grabbed Darby by the coat and tried to shake him. He might as well have grabbed a tree.

"Take it easy, Bolivar," Darby said, removing the superintendent's hands. "I'd never write anything that would hurt the Pony Express unless I knew it to be fact."

"Then what are you trying to do?"

Darby straightened his coat. "I'm not a detective. But I noticed the shells and something else."

"Such as?"

"The two bodies we dragged out from inside the cabin. Did you look at them closely?"

"Yes. They were burnt to hell!"

"True. But one very important fact stood out: they weren't dressed."

Bolivar's jaw sagged wide open. "Can you prove it?" he stammered.

"Sure." Darby held up his forefinger and started to count. "One, they didn't have their boots on, remember?"

Bolivar nodded.

"Two, they didn't have their pants on and . . ."

"How do you know that?" the superintendent asked quickly.

"Because their belts and guns were found across the

room. And three, they were bare-chested and bare-headed."

"A guess!" Bolivar shouted, almost in triumph.

"No, I'm afraid not. If they'd been wearing coats or shirts, we'd have found unburned material under their outstretched bodies where the flames couldn't reach."

Darby took a deep breath and continued. "Like it or not, Bolivar, those two men were undressed. And *I* think it was because of the squaws."

"That's preposterous!"

Darby was starting to get angry himself. Bolivar Roberts couldn't seem to understand the implications. Either that, or he was being stubborn.

"Then *you* explain it," he argued. "And answer this. Why *were* they undressed at that time of day? And what about the jewelry? If the Indians had pulled the bodies inside, they'd have searched for anything valuable, or edible, because Numaga told us his people are hungry. So why didn't they take the beads, shells, and especially this silver?"

"Make your point, Darby," Bolivar sighed after thinking about it for several minutes. "I can tell you're way ahead of me, and I'm too concerned about the future of this operation to catch up."

"All right," Darby began, "here is my theory. Admittedly, it lacks proof; yet, it's the only plausible explanation. The two strangers were characters of the foulest kind. They were naked with the Indian women."

"My men would never allow that."

"Agreed," Darby nodded. "So what does that tell you?"

Bolivar's head popped up, his eyelids shuttered. "It means they were killed by the strangers instead of the Paiutes." His face came alive. "It would explain *why* the Indians burned the station."

"Of course it would," Darby exclaimed with fervor. "It would account for everything."

Bolivar raised his hand. "Just a minute," he cautioned. "It wouldn't account for the arrows in my employees."

Darby scowled. Bolivar was right. If the two unknowns had killed the station tenders, they'd have done it with guns, not bows and arrows. And they'd never have ravaged the squaws if they'd known a band of Paiutes was nearby.

The hope he'd seen in Bolivar was dashed and the superintendent stood crestfallen.

"I still think I've explained it correctly," Darby insisted.

"It sounded good for a few minutes. But, if we can't explain the arrows that killed my station tenders, we'll never convince the people in town that Numaga didn't approve this massacre."

Darby needed to think. Something, some part of the puzzle was missing. There *had* to be an explanation. True, maybe there hadn't been women inside. Perhaps the strangers suffered an accident and were recovering in bed. It would explain their lack of clothes at that hour of the day. But that was unlikely, damnit! An even wilder speculation than his own theory. He kicked a rock and sent it flying. "Something *is* missing. We've got to find it."

"Darby, listen. I know what you're trying to do with all this squaw talk and everything. At first, I misjudged your intentions and I apologize for that. Now, I'm ready to admit I don't understand what those two unidentified men were doing inside and undressed. Maybe they were sick."

"I thought of that," Darby admitted.

"All right. But the point is, my employees *were* killed by Indians, and this station *was* burned to the ground. We can't avoid those truths. My God! There's Indian pony tracks and moccasin prints all over this yard."

"Something *is* missing."

"Of course, and the answers you need died with these men. Now, all we can do is ride back to Carson City and get help."

Darby whirled. "Think, Bolivar. All you'll get is a mob intent on war. You're the one who told me what to expect on returning to Carson City empty-handed."

"I'll try to stop it. Maybe we can talk to Numaga again. Ask him to produce those responsible." Bolivar lifted his hands in a despairing gesture. "What else can we do?"

"We can look around. Maybe you can read signs. Try, damnit! Perhaps someone in the hills witnessed the fire. Certainly the smoke would have been visible for miles. It's possible someone saw it and came to investigate." Bolivar looked skeptical.

"Well, isn't it possible? Are you so ready to just let the blood pour over this territory?"

"No."

"Then let's search for the truth before we go back."

"Very well," Bolivar decided, "we'll spend an hour. One hour. Then we must return to Carson City. If the townsfolk hear about this from some wild-eyed stranger, there's no telling how they'll react. I've got to be the one who makes the announcement. Goddamnit, I'm responsible!"

Darby glanced away. Bolivar's nerves were wiretight. The man appeared ten years older than he had yesterday. And he was right: the responsibility did rest on his shoulders. Darby himself was merely a witness to a grim piece of history. Yet, he couldn't help thinking his role allowed him a more objective view. His active mind wasn't crippled by passion and, therefore, was able to function calmly and efficiently. Some things about this Williams Station massacre just didn't fit.

"You want to ride or walk?" Bolivar asked.

Darby's backside ached mightily and there were chafed places inside his knees and along his calves. He viewed the Pony Express horse with apprehension. It looked fresh now. Fresh enough to run like hell the moment he mounted. "Let's walk," he offered hopefully. "We can't afford to miss any tracks."

"All right. But it will mean we can cover less ground. And the one hour stands."

"Then let's separate. If I see anything, I'll call."

"You won't. I wish I felt different, but we're searching for something that isn't to be found."

Darby took off walking as quickly as his short, powerful, and blistered legs would move. Maybe Bolivar was right. Yet, given the reception they'd face in town, what did they have to lose?

* * *

Down near the river, where the sand was wet, they found two sets of boot prints. They were clear and Darby's hopes soared. "Look at the size of this one," he said, placing his own foot down in the impression.

It was at least two inches longer than his own. To be sure, Darby found it was precisely the width of three fingers longer than his own footprint. He stepped aside and put his weight down. Then, finding a twig, he measured the depth of his print against the other. It was deeper by a quarter of an inch.

He stood up. "Whoever made that print was a taller and even heavier man than I. He was huge."

Bolivar nodded. "There are some giants in this country. Especially some of those foreign miners who work up in Virginia City. Why, I saw a Welshman who must have been six and a half feet tall and as thick as you are."

Darby nodded absently. He was thinking of another giant. One who had planted an oversized boot in his ribs only a few weeks ago.

"Come on," Bolivar said impatiently. "Let's follow these tracks and see where they lead."

Darby held his suspicions. Up to now, he'd thrown out about all Bolivar could stand. But, as he followed, his memory filed away the length and depth of that boot print. He had a debt to pay to Claude Tulley, and he'd make darned sure the man's boot planted itself in the dirt instead of in his ribs next time. It was a meeting he eagerly awaited.

The tracks went downriver, then crossed and continued up into the hills. He and Bolivar were so intent upon watching them that they stumbled right into a pair of rifle sights.

"Hold it! Put your hands up," came the shouted order. "One false move and you're maggot meat."

Darby dropped his shotgun and punched the sky, and the superintendent did the same. Up ahead, he could see two rifles. They protruded from the rocks like the evil witches' wands of childhood fairytales, capable of making things disappear—things such as their lives.

"What do you want?"

"To talk," Bolivar shouted.

"Then do it!"

Darby relaxed. He lowered his thick arms a fraction of an inch. That was a mistake. A rifle bullet seared the flesh between his splayed fingers. He reached for the clouds as a man dying of thirst who might wring them free of water.

"One more time and it's your gizzard, fat man."

Darby bristled with anger. Fat man! Why, he'd show them. Yet, his eyes rolled up in their sockets and he saw blood dripping down his hand, rivering across his wrist, and seeping wetly under the cuff of his white shirt. He'd *never* get it clean. The shirt was ruined. Still, better a shirt than his gizzard.

"You all right?" Bolivar whispered out of one side of his mouth.

"Yes. Merely angry."

"Well, don't lose your temper."

"Ask them if they saw the Indians," Darby hissed.

"My name is Bolivar Roberts and . . ."

"Spell it."

"Huh?"

"I said spell it. You keep yammerin' and we'll scratch it on a wooden cross after the buryin'."

Bolivar swallowed noisily and Darby licked his lips. "Bolivar Roberts is the superintendent of the Pony Express," he croaked. "Surely, you gentlemen have heard of the venture."

"Who the hell are you?"

"I'm a writer."

"Rider?" There was a round of chuckles. "Why, you'd sway an elephant's backbone."

"Not rider, writer," he screeched in exasperation.

"Yore wrong, dude. Yore carrion same as your friend unless you both fall to the ground and lizard on down this hill."

Bolivar thudded to the dirt, but Darby had to try once more. "Did you see the Indians burn our station? We have to know."

"What station?"

"The express station. The one down there on the

other side of the river." He turned to point and caught himself just in time as another slug buzzed past his right ear.

"For godsake, Darby, hit the dirt and let's get moving!"

"Don't see no station," the reply came floating down. "We ain't seen anything, fat man. Now, this is your last chance."

"But it's important," Darby yelled in rage.

"Must be. Even more important than yore lives."

Darby dropped. The implication was clear. There would be no more conversation. The two prospectors weren't interested in talk. He took off on his hands and knees, following the rapidly moving backside of the superintendent. Before he'd scrambled a hundred yards, he'd snagged and ripped the knees out of both trouser legs.

Blast. First the shirt, now the pants. And for what? To be insulted and shot at?

When they finally rounded the hill and were out of sight, both men sagged with exhaustion and gratitude for their lives. Darby was out of breath, his lungs emptying and refilling in staccato bursts. "I'm . . . I'm going to go back," he gasped.

Bolivar looked at him redly. "Not today, you're not. Damnit, man, you almost got our tickets punched!"

"They were lying. They had to be. Did you see that tunnel?"

"Yeah."

"Well, it wasn't dug this morning. They've been around and they do have the answers we need. Those two can finish our puzzle."

Bolivar clawed to his feet, nipping stickers out of the palms of his hands. Then he stomped away. "Your hour is finished, Mr. Buckingham. We're riding."

Darby shook his head. Bolivar was really on the prod. It would be useless to try to talk the man into circling around and surprising those two up in the rocks. Yet, that was exactly what they should be doing.

He reluctantly followed Bolivar. Maybe it was best to leave now. The way things were going, they'd just get themselves shot trying to take those prospectors alive.

Darby cast a glance backward, forgetting they were out of sight. He *would* return. And he *would* get some answers. There was simply nowhere else to turn.

Chapter 6

"I say the time has come for action! If we let those heathen Paiutes get away with this terrible outrage, no man, woman, or child will be safe. We must strike back. Hit them hard and fast. Pluck two eyes for one."

Major William M. Ormsby, tall, fiery-eyed, leading citizen and prosperous owner of the Ormsby House, caught his breath and glared down from the second story of his hotel toward the crowd. "We must *ride* for vengeance. It is reported that the vicious Paiutes are gathering their warriors to drive the white man out of this entire territory. I say we strike now!"

"No." Bolivar Roberts argued passionately. "We must be reasonable. This is not the time to act on wild rumors and fear. We . . ."

The crowd began to hoot and jeer. Someone shoved Bolivar, and Darby caught him before he fell.

"We must organize. I'm asking every able-bodied patriot in Carson City to follow me." Ormsby's hair was disheveled, his fist clenched. He raised it to the sky, an eerie figure in the bonfire light that rose from the street below. "Will you follow me?" he implored dramatically.

The audience rocked with shouting intensity and drunkenly hoisted whiskey bottles and guns.

Darby shook his head. This was madness! Around him, people swilled liquor and danced about as though preparing for a celebration.

He had to stop this. But, even as Darby climbed up on a wagon and tried to shout them down, he knew it was too late. Where an hour before there had been shock and fear, now he saw whiskey courage.

They were united in their cry for revenge. And, soon, they would be reinforced by others who felt as they did. Even now, the call was being sent for help, to the south toward Genoa and to the east up toward Sun Mountain where the restless miners of Silver City and Virginia City would pour from the great Comstock mines. They would gather like armies in the night to crush the godless Paiute hordes.

"Listen to me," Darby pleaded, "you must not act foolishly."

Major Ormsby and the crowd jerked around and glared at the Derby Man.

"I think the Indians had provocation. We found . . ."

"Four dead whites," someone cried hoarsely. "And how many Indians?"

Shouts of anger and derision poured up at him like a giant wave of hatred. Darby tried to shout them down. "There may have been a rape of Paiute squaws!"

It wasn't what they wanted to hear. Not at all. Men grabbed his leg and yanked him down into the street. Darby swung and connected but the crowd surged over him.

"Stop it!" Ormsby cried, firing his gun into the sky. "Stop it at once."

Darby's mouth tasted of blood, and he flung the hands away as his attackers reluctantly stepped back.

"He is not our enemy. Neither is Mr. Bolivar Roberts. We must act wisely."

Darby clambered to his feet, shaking the dust away and wondering if there was a chance after all. Perhaps he'd misjudged Ormsby. But, his hope was short-lived.

Ormsby continued. "The wise thing to do, though I'm as eager as any of you, is to wait and march at daybreak."

There was a moan of disappointment. Behind Darby, someone agreed reluctantly because 'Injuns could see better than whites in the dark.'

"And the reason we must wait is that, at this very moment . . . ," he hesitated until the crowd below strained with anticipation. "At this very moment, I have received word that the valiant men of the Comstock have pledged to join our forces!" Some cheered, others applauded, but a few were too drunk to care.

"Aw, who the hell needs 'em, Majer?" a voice

slurred. "Them Paiutes are afraid to fight. All they can do is eat pine nuts. The only things they can hit with their arrows are the ducks and geese on Pyramid Lake."

The crowd roared with laughter.

"Maybe that's true," Ormsby called down with a grin, "but, gentlemen, we cannot be so selfish as to take *all* the glory. At this very moment, horses are being confiscated on the Comstock, and the miners are riding down to join us."

One of the more sober spectators called, "Those miners are crazy. They'll be too drunk to fight."

"Not so," Ormsby countered. "Mr. Archie McDonald is their captain, while, in Silver City, R.G. Watkins has been chosen to lead his volunteers."

"R.G. Watkins! Why, Major, you musta heard it wrong. R.G. is one-legged. He couldn't lead school children to the outhouse."

Ormsby stiffened. "He has a fine military record. I will be grateful to have him serve as my lieutenant. And . . . and as far as his missing leg is concerned, it is a *tribute* to his courage. It was lost in a gallant expedition under William Walker in Nicaragua."

Ormsby cleared his throat dramatically. "My friends, Mr. Watkins will lead his contingent of men into this just fight and, because of his missing leg, he will be *tied* to the saddle."

The lingering snickers and crass comments that had been circulating died at this bit of news. Tied to his saddle. Now, that *was* brassy. Almost at once, toasts were raised to the courage of Watkins all around.

Beside Darby, Boliver Roberts muttered. "That's a lie. Watkins was in the Navy during the Mexican War. He lost his leg in a San Diego street brawl back in '51."

Darby nodded wearily. Why should Watkins's past be held up to the cold light of truth? Nothing else was.

A horse wheeled around the corner of the Ormsby House and its rider shouted, "Mr. Howard Clayton has agreed to lead the brave men of Genoa, Major Ormsby."

Darby stiffened and glanced at Bolivar Roberts who simply nodded. "The very same, I'm afraid."

"Bravo!" Ormsby cried, raising his fist in anticipated victory. Then, addressing the excited mob below, he proclaimed, "That's it, my gallant friends of Carson City. Tomorrow we will march to avenge this despicable outrage."

Ormsby watched them ignite into a mass cheer. Then, like a tolerant schoolmaster, he patted the air for silence. "Gentlemen, we cannot fail. Our cause is just. And the spoils of our victory will be no more than due punishment. I have a slogan in mind. If you approve, it will be our rallying cry."

"Tell us! Tell us!"

"It is simply, 'An Indian for breakfast and a pony to ride.' "

Guns were drawn and fired. Hats, and even a few almost emptied whiskey bottles, sailed into the air while Darby Buckingham and Boliver Roberts slowly walked away.

Darby was going back. Back to the charred ashes of Williams Station. He couldn't remain in Carson City and wait for the bloody news of the Pyramid Lake battle that would soon take place. One hundred and five men, whom Major Ormsby called an army, had galloped from town. To Darby, they were simply drunken rabble, hunting for excitement and glory at little or no personal cost. From the conversation of the night before, most of the citizens didn't expect to fire a shot. The Paiutes would turn it into a human fox hunt.

In a way, Darby hoped Numaga would run. Perhaps, when the long ride was over and the whiskey burned out of their stomachs, the volunteers would begin to think. Major Ormsby would have had his brief dance with glory and be able to claim he'd chased the entire Paiute Nation into the desert. His ego, and that of the Comstock region, would be appeased, and no blood would be lost by either side.

But, most importantly, it would give Darby time to unravel the mystery behind the Williams Station massacre. And he needed time.

Darby unsaddled his horse in the cottonwoods beside the burned rubble and hitched up his pants. All this riding was causing him to lose weight. That made him unhappy because his family took pride in being robust. To Darby, weight meant strength. And by the measurement of his belt, he ruefully concluded he'd lost ten or fifteen pounds. If that kept up, he was going to need the services of a tailor very soon.

When a Buckingham could look down his chin and see the toes of his shoes, he was underweight. And, as Darby reached up and pulled his saddle off, he could clearly see his toes. He glanced over at the pack horse he'd brought and felt encouragement. In those packs, he'd stashed away enough food, hard candy, and imported brandy to last a week.

In fact, he didn't expect to remain longer than two days. His objective was of dual nature. He would try to establish conversation with the nearby prospectors on the one hand and, on the other, he was going to be waiting for Pony Bob Haslam. The pack horse, while appearing calm and plodding, was really a pony express mount.

When Haslam came through, he was to switch horses and ride on to Carson City. Meanwhile, Bolivar Roberts was preparing supplies and attempting to hire replacement tenders for Williams Station. But the superintendent hadn't been having much luck in recruiting. The reasons were obvious.

Darby rested until late afternoon before climbing into the hills. This time, he was prepared. In one fist, he carried a Winchester rifle and in the other his shotgun. Tucked under his belt was a pistol. If he had to rely on the Winchester or the pistol, he was in for big trouble. But the two prospectors did not know he couldn't shoot. Darby hoped being armed to the teeth would make them decide he meant business.

They'd better, because he did. If a war could be prevented, Darby would take whatever steps necessary to see that it was stopped. And besides, Judge John Cradebaugh of Carson City had listened to their story. He'd told Darby and Bolivar to bring him evidence so that steps might be taken to negotiate a peace. Cradebaugh had also reminded the writer that time was of the essence.

Darby flattened and began to "lizard," as they'd so aptly termed it, through the sagebrush. He was doing quite well and guessed the prospectors' camp was right ahead. They'd never . . .

With his eyes focused ahead, he overlooked the scorpion. But then, he'd never been warned that Nevada sagebrush teems with the hateful critters. So Darby placed his hand right on top of a big one.

The pain was violent. Excruciating. Darby bellowed and his eyes rolled. The scorpion twitched, raised its tail for another sting. Darby leapt up into the air and opened up on the repulsive creature with both barrels of his shotgun.

The roar was deafening. The gunfire obliterated the scorpion and left a great depression in the earth between Darby's feet.

He grabbed his wrist and squeezed as though he might force the venom out of his body. Pain, like a molten river of lava, flowed up his arm and he staggered.

"Drop your guns and stretch for the sky, fat man."

Darby groaned, cursed himself, the scorpion, and the two rifle-toting prospectors. "Blast . . . blast . . . triple blast!"

His fingers were becoming numb. "A damned scorpion bit me," he gritted.

The prospectors lowered their rifles. They were like brothers, as identical in size and appearance as twins—old, wrinkled, tough, and smelly. "Let's see. Stick your paw out."

Darby obeyed. One poked the other in the ribs. "Maybe the scorpion saved us the price of a bullet," he chuckled.

But the other was peering at Darby's quivering fingers and rapidly swelling fist. "We got to help him."

"Why? He was sneaking up to kill us. Maybe Clay . . ."

Darby glanced up. "What did you say?" he gasped. "Did you say, Clayton?"

A veil dropped over the speaker's eyes. "I didn't say nothin'," he swore. "What the hell do you want?"

"Help," Darby stated quietly.

"Evans, we can't let him die."

"Aw, he won't. Scorpions usually just make you sick. Only kill you sometimes." He gripped his rifle and raised it until the barrel was on Darby's chest. "I'm more worried he *ain't* goin' to die."

Darby already felt sick. "Then you'd better use that rifle," he choked. "Because, if I *do* live, I'm coming back again and again until I get some answers."

"What answers? We don't know nothin'. All we want to do is be left alone."

Darby's legs began to tremble, and he sagged to his knees. "There's over a hundred men riding up to Pyramid Lake this day. They're going to attack the Paiutes because of what happened down at that Pony Express station."

"Good," Evans swore. "I hope they kill every damned one of 'em. Me and my partner would rest a lot easier."

"But the Paiutes had a reason," Darby groaned. "You saw those women. You must have."

Hank Brown started to speak, but Evans shot him a hard look that froze the words. "We ain't seen nothin'."

"Why are you so afraid? Do you want innocent blood shed? Tell me the truth."

Darby's head began to spin. He rolled sideways, feeling a torrent of sweat break out across his body.

"We got to help him."

Evans lowered his rifle. "All right," he conceded reluctantly. "We'll make up a poultice and get him back on his feet. He'll be strong enough by tomorrow to walk outa here."

"And if he ain't?"

"Then he'll be dead and our troubles are over."

At first light, they helped Darby to his feet. "Can you make it down to the river?"

Darby nodded. He felt drained and wobbly. Up the underside of one arm was a bluish tinge. His ears rang and his stomach felt burned out from some kind of medicine they'd given him twice in the night.

"Don't come back," Evans warned. "We didn't see nothin', and we ain't sayin' nothin' either."

Darby inhaled, then exhaled slowly. "I think you *did* see what happened," he told them. "And you recognized Clayton and Tulley. Now, you're afraid to speak."

"It's healthier to mind your own business in this country, Buckingham. Maybe, being a writer and all, you can't understand that, but it's the gospel truth."

"I can understand it," Darby sighed. "But you don't seem to realize what's at stake here. I've tried to explain and . . ."

"What's at stake is our goddamn lives, Mister! That's what we're talking about."

Darby turned to leave. "All right, but I hope your conscience is clear, knowing you could have prevented slaughter and did not."

"Git," Evans hissed. "We got work to do."

Darby shook his head in despair. He was no closer to answering the mystery than he'd been two days ago. And, because of that, fifty miles above Reno, both red and white men were going to die.

Their saddlebags clanked with whiskey bottles, and they marked a trail north with shattered empties.

Claude Tulley was scared. That first night they camped, the wind had come up cold and biting and later, while they'd huddled around their campfires, it had begun to snow. Snow in May wasn't unheard of in this high desert land, but still it seemed a bad omen to Tulley. He hadn't slept much that night. The icy wind blasted through the trees and he shivered, thinking of what lay ahead.

In the early evening, Tulley had listened to the men debate the wisdom of going on. At least thirty of the riders were openly afraid, now that they were actually going into hostile territory. They'd argued that the U.S. Army was better suited to defeat Numaga. After all, that was what they were paid to do.

Claude Tulley remained silent, but he desperately

wished Clayton hadn't opened his damned mouth and volunteered to lead the Genoa detachment. Otherwise, he'd be riding out of this country and leaving these fools to play their deadly game.

As they rode ever closer, certain things bothered the hell out of Tulley: their force was poorly armed, poorly mounted, and still drinking heavily. To make things worse, he'd discovered that Major Ormsby wasn't a leader at all. Each of the four contingents of volunteers insisted on taking their orders from the man they'd elected. So, if they got into a real scrape, Tulley knew it was going to be every man for himself.

Each mile they traveled increased Tulley's doubts. The wind kept moaning. And straight ahead, the prints of unshod hooves of Paiute ponies drew them ever closer, and he couldn't help wondering why the Indians had left such a clear trail into their stronghold.

"Don't you think Ormsby oughta send scouts up ahead?" he asked.

Clayton's skin was the color of wax. He looked terrible. The cold, long hours in the saddle and the whiskey had aged him in just twenty-four hours. "Shut up," the old man snapped. "Me and the major know what we're doing."

"You'd better," Tulley vowed crossly. "It's our lives you're gambling with."

Clayton stared ahead and Tulley fell back to the rear. Yet, twenty minutes later, he saw his boss ride up and speak to the major. Shortly afterward, Ormsby called a halt and asked for volunteers to scout ahead.

They were close now, very close. Before them lay the Truckee River and, just a few miles farther, the great dead lake which drank the river's flow.

The scouts returned. Yes, they'd seen Indians. Two of them. But there were hundreds of pony tracks. Ormsby nodded, gave the signal, and they moved on.

When they reached the flat land of the river valley, Tulley noticed they were now in a pocket. He began to sweat, though the air was cold. To the southeast, he could look back at the steep trail they'd just descended. To the west, there was a high bluff which would be impossible to scale. To the south, he saw the river gush-

ing down through a narrow and impassable canyon.
And straight ahead yawned the wide valley funneling
into Pyramid Lake. If we're going to turn back, he
thought, it better be now.

But they didn't. Once more, Ormsby gave the order
to advance. There was a light snow on the ground and
their horses moved silently. Yet, Tulley could feel a
thousand eyes watching, and his own heartbeat
pumped in his ears, and fear teased the ridges of his
backbone.

Suddenly, just ahead, where the late afternoon sun
burned, a line of more than one hundred mounted
braves appeared against the skyline. A huge chief carrying what looked like a war ax began to ride back and
forth.

"Let's charge," Ormsby cried.

But Captain McDonald, head of the Virginia City
volunteers, disagreed and urged a retreat down to the
cottonwoods near the river. They'd be protected on
one flank by the river and by an open plain on the
other.

"I said charge!" Ormsby screamed, whipping his
mount forward.

Tulley froze. At most, thirty men from Carson City
raced after their leader. Tulley saw their already weary
horses, thin and weakened by a long winter, stagger up
toward the braves.

Almost reluctantly, the chief signaled a retreat, and
Ormsby and his followers billowed with confidence,
and they began to shout over and over, "An Indian for
breakfast and a pony to ride. Yee-haw!"

But, as they neared the summit, it happened. Out of
the brush sprang the waiting Paiutes. They opened fire
from both sides and Tulley saw the thirty convulse like
a wounded snake. Their rallying motto dissolved as
men tried to control their horses on the treacherous
hillside and fire at the swarming Indians.

Through the gunfire, Major Ormsby could be heard
yelling for an orderly retreat to the cottonwoods. But
he was too late. Already the thirty were halved and
those who remained in the saddle were flying back
down the hill, scattering like leaves in a storm.

Tulley yanked his horse around. He was getting out of here. Not to the cottonwoods, but back up the southeast trail they'd just descended. Before he could sink spurs, however, another line of Indians appeared to block his retreat.

He swung his horse in a full circle. The sounds of dying men filled his ears. Where to run? Everywhere, he saw more Indians. Terror froze his mind as riders milled around in chaos.

"Fall back to the trees! Fall back and regroup!" Clayton shouted as the survivors of Ormsby's men poured down among them.

Tulley was in the forefront. Just three hundred yards ahead, the cottonwood grove promised life and sanctuary. But then, out of those trees, a swarm of Paiutes arose.

Tulley felt gutted by fear. They were going to die.

"The arroyo! Make a stand in the arroyo."

He pulled the reins so viciously his horse almost fell as the entire group veered toward the poor cover.

The Indians were charging, yelling, firing rifles and using their powerful short bows with killing accuracy.

Ormsby kept screaming for the men to hold their position and make a stand. But, to do so, they'd have to release their horses. And, to Claude Tulley, that was madness. Suicide.

"Oh God," he sobbed. "I don't want to be scalped."

So, he did what everyone else did. He ran—ran while the sound of bullets and arrows thudded into flesh and the Indian shrieks filled his ears.

A brave leapt for him. The man seemed to material-ize from nothing. Tulley shot him at close range but the Indian's body fell under his horse's legs and the an-imal went crazy. Two seconds, perhaps three, were lost as he struggled to get it under control. By then, it was too late. A rifle slug knocked his mount to its knees and Tulley kicked free and rolled, firing as two more Paiutes sprinted at him with thick obsidian knives.

He shot them both, yet he was so terrified he kept pulling the trigger until it clicked empty.

Behind him, the volunteers who'd dismounted to make their stand in the arroyo with Ormsby now realized they were being deserted to die. They began running away on foot, grabbing whatever frightened mule or horse they could reach, pleading for their friends to help.

Tulley hurled his empty gun away. One rider, a boy in his teens, was hunched over in his saddle. Tulley jumped at him but the animal shied away and went racing by. Another rider followed, and Tulley leapt once more. He grabbed for the bit and held on, dragging the wild-eyed mount to a standstill while its rider swore at him to let go. Tulley grabbed the man with one hand and threw him screaming into the sagebrush.

He swung into the saddle and drove spurs. The Indians ahead put up a withering fire, and Tulley was forced to rein away and circle the meadow. He saw Major Ormsby still holding his position with a few others. The major was blood-soaked, struggling to lift his gun, and all the while he shouted to the crazed survivors to hold their position and to the scattering riders to release their horses and collect behind him.

To hell with that! Nothing on earth could have convinced Tulley that his only chance didn't depend on flight.

Some of those around Tulley made a break for the river and Tulley almost followed. But at the last moment, he reined his animal away when he saw how the floundering mounts were swept downcurrent toward a line of excited warriors who ran along the riverbank waving battle axes.

And then Clayton passed him, yelling for the survivors to take to the cottonwoods. It was their only chance. Again and again he shouted, until Ormsby and the few who remained standing beside the wounded major realized there was no other choice. Clayton was right, and Tulley knew he wasn't going out alone. He had no alternative but to spur toward the trees.

Quickly, they fought their way through the Indians to reach the cottonwoods. And finally, when all seemed lost, their terror was replaced by a grim determination to sell their lives as dearly as possible. A few were hysterical enough to throw down their weapons and run for death, but they *were* few and, as Tulley reached the cottonwoods, desperate hand-to-hand battles were being fought on the carpet of dead leaves.

Tulley joined that fight. He scooped up a fallen comrade's rifle and made it smoke. When the bullets were gone, he went after the Indians using the weapon as a club. Something had snapped inside the giant. With his terrible strength and awesome size, he swirled through the battle in a killing rage.

For a moment, he found himself alone under the trees. Blood was rolling into his eyes from a wound he didn't feel.

"Mount up," Ormsby cried. "We're going to take the trail out!"

The big man staggered, still gripping the empty rifle by its barrel. An arm grabbed him. Dazed, he pivoted, lifting the weapon. "Tulley," Clayton shouted. "I got two horses. Let's go!"

He did as he was told. Out of the trees they burst. Straight for the southeastern pass that had led them into this carnage. But this time they stayed in a tight-moving body.

Ormsby was in front, bent over his saddle and swaying precariously. Arrows winged through them, winnowing their numbers in a coldly random way.

For the first time in his life, Tulley wished he were a small man, a runt even. He lay as flat as he could over his horse's neck and willed himself to be small. On his left, along the ridgeline, he spied Paiutes whipping their mounts, frantically trying to cut off the escape route, a pass where only a handful of warriors braced themselves and waited.

As they surged up out of the river bottom, he kept his mount squarely in the center of the pack because those on the flanks were dying faster.

It seemed forever before they reached the trail leading out. Yet, now, for the first time, Tulley realized they did have a chance to escape, if his horse didn't fall and its heart didn't burst.

The volunteers cut the handful of braves who tried to block their path as a scythe going through brittle grain stalks. Then, the pass narrowed and the riders funneled upward, almost in single file.

Ormsby shouted for help to cover the retreat. Tulley glanced the other way and so did Clayton. When they finally reached the plateau above, Tulley's horse slammed into a milling band of riders.

"My God!" someone whispered. "Look."

A quarter of a mile below, Tulley saw a riderless horse sprawled across the trail. The major had its reins and was trying to pull it up. Then, Ormsby heard the Indians close behind. Tulley watched the man drop the reins, lift his pistol with two hands and begin firing. One brave pitched from his animal, but the torrent behind him washed over the major. Arms, axes, and those terrible obsidian blades rose and fell.

It was a horse race now. The amazing thing to Tulley was that so many had survived. Of the hundred and five, he estimated there were sixty who rode for their lives across the desert. But it wasn't a fair race. Their horses were exhausted, while the Indians who closed in from behind rode fresh animals.

And, one by one, the stragglers were pulled down by their shrieking pursuers. Tulley felt his own horse beginning to falter.

"Clayton," he sobbed, "my horse. It's starting to fade. Clayton, they're going to catch me!"

They were riding stirrup to stirrup. But the old man's horse was carrying half the weight and looked twice as strong.

"Clayton!"

"I can't help you, damnit." The old man seemed like a ghost rider in the night. Tulley saw him raise his whip and knew what his boss was doing, saving his own skin if he could.

Tulley punched his faltering horse with spurs and it leapt to catch up. Then, the giant reached out and encircled Clayton's scrawny neck, dragging him out of the saddle.

"No," the old man choked as he slid between the two running horses. "Please!"

"Sorry, boss," Tulley gritted, "but you've lived longer than I have."

He let him fall. Tulley changed horses at a dead run and started to outdistance his pursuers. Behind, the screams rose and fell. He didn't care. He'd save his own scalp—if he could.

Chapter 7

Through the days that followed, Darby spent a lot of time soaking his melon-sized hand in the river. Gradually the swelling reduced, though it was hard to tell because his fingers and palm were abnormally short and thick anyway. He considered himself fortunate it was his left hand, and that he could continue to work on his novel. So far, he was still in the note-taking stage of the work, and he tried to set down on paper all of the events he'd seen thus far as accurately as possible.

Besides working on his notes, Darby ate prodigiously. After all, the scorpion had made him sick enough to miss two meals in a row, and he was genuinely alarmed at his shrinking waistline. The day after being stung, he consumed an entire pickled ham, three cans of peaches, four tins of sardines, a loaf of bread, a pound of delicious cheese, and washed it all down with a river-chilled bottle of brandy. By the end of the day, he was feeling very content indeed and took no small measure of satisfaction when his belt had to be let out two notches.

Yet, after that first great gastronomical binge, Darby knew he would have to go a little easier on the feeding. His job was to hold the station for Pony Bob Haslam and, with all the uncertainty about the Indians, there was some question as to exactly when the rider would arrive.

Once he appeared, Darby would escort the man back to Carson City. He'd have to travel fast—and light. That's why he wanted to consume all the food he'd packed in, or else the chosen delicacies would be left behind. A terrible waste.

By the third day, he was getting anxious. Haslam should have come by now and Darby was down to one ham, two pounds of licorice candy, and river water for drink. If something didn't happen soon, he'd be in a fix. Maybe he'd have to resort to the mercy of the two prospectors and beg, God forbid, for his food.

The thought made him shudder. He decided it might be wise to pay them a sociable visit, openly this time. Besides, he was still convinced that the prospectors had witnessed the true story behind the charred remains called Williams Station. And, sooner or later, by force or whatever charm he could muster, they *had* to be made to testify before the authorities.

On his way up the hillside, he silently cursed his luck for having to deal with two such pigheaded and stubborn men. And he kept an eye to the ground for scorpions. Several times, he thought fondly of New York City where, at this hour of the day, he used to bask in a green, tree-shaded park, feed the greedy pigeons, or visit a favorite art gallery which suited his pleasure.

Failing that, and taking a giant step down on the scale of comfort and sophistication, he would gladly have settled for his comfortable John C. Fremont suite in Running Springs, Wyoming; and, of course, the good and robust Dolly Beavers to play her provocative but harmless games.

Trudging up that brush-covered hill, wondering if scorpions possessed the agility to leap up and stab his legs, and thinking about those two reprehensible old prospectors with which he was forced to plead, Darby Buckingham had a few doubts about promises made that he would be only a spectator in this historic play which was unfolding. Correction, he decided: probable tragedy.

Some spectator. Hostile Indians, enraged scorpions, and two crazy old codgers.

Darby neared the crest of the hill and took a deep breath. Behind him, he could gaze down on the Carson River and the line of trees with their bright new leaves beginning to sprout. So peaceful. Deceptively peaceful. He shaded his eyes and studied the panorama to the east where Pony Bob Haslam would appear first as a thin trail of dust across the wasteland. But there was no trail of dust. He sighed. At least that meant no Indians.

Darby resisted the temptation to return to his camp. The licorice called strongly.

"Hello the camp."

They charged out of their mine as if it were inhabited by a grizzly bear. Two men, streaking for the brush, diving headlong for cover and rising to fire.

"Don't shoot," Darby yelled, waving his hands overhead. "I'm unarmed."

"It's the fat man," Hank Brown spat in disgust. He stood up, looking mad enough to shoot anyway.

Darby kept his hands overhead and tried to make his voice sound ingratiating. "Good afternoon, my friends."

"What do you want *now*?"

He curbed his disappointment well. "Nothing really," he shrugged, wondering if he might lower his hands. It was difficult to be cordial in such a pose.

"Then git out of here!"

"How's the digging today?" he offered good-naturedly.

They glared in silence. It wasn't going to work. A poor opening remark at best.

"Git." Brown raised his Winchester menacingly.

Darby backpedaled. "Wait a minute. "I'm . . . I'm hungry."

"Hungry," Evans swore. "You're in shape to hibernate for the winter."

The other guffawed much more loudly than Darby thought necessary. Still, if the childish joke improved their miserable attitude concerning strangers, it wasn't all bad.

"I have money," he offered. "And I'd be more than willing to buy—at a large profit to you, of course—a few edibles."

Brown's eyelids lowered. "How much money you carrying?"

His intent was clear and, inwardly, Darby stiffened. After all, he'd tried on three occasions to negotiate their trust and friendship. True, they had doctored him from the scorpion's sting, but they'd also propelled him out of camp while he was still quite unwell.

He made his decision and was glad. No more pandering to their insensibilities. It was time to act forcibly. But that required getting in close enough to disarm them.

"Oh," he said, "I've probably no more than a hundred dollars or so in my wallet."

"A hundred dollars! Why, come on down, Mister . . . I forgot your handle." They both lay their rifles against a pinion tree.

"Buckingham. Darby Buckingham." Then, shamelessly, he felt compelled to add, "Better known out west as the Derby Man."

They exchanged looks, but said nothing until he stood between them.

"Well, Mister Derby Man, let's see the color of yore money. Then we can talk prices. We got beans, dried possum, some cornmeal, and some whiskey."

Darby reached inside his coat for his wallet, and, just as he'd suspected, the two prospectors reached for their revolvers.

Before they quite understood what was happening, Darby grabbed their beards and rocked their heads together. The dull THUNK set them to struggling, so he yanked their heads together a couple of more times for good measure until they were cross-eyed and wobbly.

The two men began to reel around in small circles, making funny sounds. Darby collected their weapons and gently led them back to their mine and pushed them inside. Both slid down and clutched their heads in pain.

"Now," Darby said, "I apologize for resorting to force. However, your intent was low and dishonorable. I'm genuinely concerned about the matter of Williams Station."

"Go to hell!" one cried. They were beginning to revive.

Darby scowled so ferociously that his thick black eyebrows met. "Mind your tongues or I'll come in there and crack your skulls together until you babble like children."

"No. No," they shouted in unison, while scrambling deeper into the mine.

"Then tell me what you know about Williams Station."

They retreated until he couldn't see them anymore but only heard their frantic whispering.

"Well," he demanded impatiently, "what's it to be?"

He recognized Evans's voice first, and it was almost pleading. "Mister Derby Man, we *can't* say nothin'."

"Why not?"

"Because . . ."

"Shut up!" hissed the other. "Because it wouldn't be healthy, that's why."

Darby shook with frustration. They *had* seen the massacre, only they were too scared to admit it.

"I'll protect you," he called into the tunnel.

"Hogwash and horsefeathers you will."

"Then . . . then, I'll get help. Please. You're the only ones who can avert a war."

"Leave us alone. We got nothing to say."

"Damn you fools. I'm coming in and I'll . . ."

"You do and we'll gut you, Derby Man. We don't want to, but we'll use these knives if we're cornered."

Darby, half-crouched and preparing to enter, hesitated.

"It's dark back here," Evans called menacingly, "and we know how to use our stickers. Don't make us do it."

"Blast," Darby swore. He had them backed up like trapped animals. They *would* resort to the blade. He stood up, clipping the back of his head painfully on the tunnel's lip. "Blast!"

"You goin'?"

"Yes," Darby snapped angrily. "But I *won't* give up on you. I'll keep returning until you either kill me or I strangle the truth from your mouths."

There was a long silence. "If yore hungry, take what you need and leave your money in the grub sack."

"Go to hell!" Darby roared.

"Go fish then, you big galoot."

He rubbed the depression in his scalp. Maybe he would.

*   *   *

It was late afternoon. Still no Pony Bob Haslam. Darby had thought about fishing and decided it was as good a way as any to pass time profitably. More out of spite than necessity, he'd rummaged through the prospectors' provisions and found fishing line and hooks.

Now, he undressed, laid his black coat, trousers, and shoes on a rock and unbuttoned his shirt. There was a dark ring around the starched white collar that reminded him he needed a bath.

Very well, then, he would bathe as he fished. Already he could almost smell the catch roasting on his fire. True, without the spices and sauces, he couldn't hope to duplicate the wonderful New York seafood he loved, but the thought of eating another ham offered no appeal.

It took him almost twenty minutes of disagreeable scrounging before he found the worm. By then, the bottoms of his feet were covered with cuts and bruises. Darby cleaned the worm, then ruthlessly rammed the hook through its wiggling body. He studied the water and chose a good rock upon which he could fish and bathe. Despite the unforeseen difficulties, he was determined to see this thing through.

He ventured forth. "Damn the ham. Rout the trout," he chanted happily.

But the rocks were slick with moss. The first he stepped upon twisted meanly and sent him staggering into the icy river, fighting for his balance.

"Brrrrr," he gasped, seeing his feet turn ivory with the cold. He bent over and started forward much more cautiously now. Darby trusted no rock to support his considerable weight. Each step was taken with care and a gradual easing down until it proved its trustworthiness.

Stepping upon the broad rock he'd chosen, Darby plunked down with relief and no little pride. He dangled his injured palm into the current and decided to hold off on the bathing until he'd landed his meal.

The worm had expired and now seemed small and unappetizing bait. Still, it would have to do. Perhaps, he thought hopefully, a trout was not very discriminating. Somehow, though, the six feet of twine had become tangled. For a few moments, he fumbled with the mess; then his lips curled in disgust. While Buckinghams were legendary for their appetites and strength, they were cursed with thick and clumsy fingers. In his distinguished line of ancestors, no Buckingham had ever been a craftsman. No matter—it was enough that he could adequately manipulate a quill or cap his bottle of ink.

Oh well, he thought, three feet of line should be ample if the trout were paying attention to the worm. He dropped the sagging bait into the current and waited. And waited. And waited. Finally, when he was going stiff and thinking of ham, he saw the quick gray green beauty undulating beneath a nearby rock.

Darby drew in his breath with appreciation. It was a whale—at least three feet long and as thick as his forearm. "Come closer," he whispered imploringly. But the ignorant fish refused to budge; it only waved its great fan-shaped tail to the currents and eddies.

Darby leaned as far over the water as he dared. If only the line hadn't tangled. The wretched worm would be tickling those puckered fish lips. Just a few more inches and then surely the trout must take notice.

Darby stretched as far . . . no, farther than seemed possible. His eyes were glued to the indolent behemoth so fixedly that . . .

The gunfire propelled him forward and launched him over the big trout, making it show life. Darby struck the water and bellowed in shock. His breath seemed to freeze in his lungs and his heart convulsed and shriveled in his chest.

"Ahhh," he roared, thrashing madly in two feet of shivering hell. He flopped crazily from one rock to another on his way to shore, spluttering, cursing his luck, and hearing the gunshots grow ever closer.

Then he saw the cause of his misfortune and, instantly, his teeth ceased to chatter. For there, less than two miles away and storming in from the east was Pony Bob Haslam. And right behind came a howling band of Paiute Indians.

Even as Darby stood almost naked and with rivulets of Sierra-snow runoff funneling his shivering bulk, he saw Pony Bob lean around in his saddle and fire.

Darby forgot about the trout, the ham, his clothes—everything. In moments, they would be upon him. There was no time for anything save escape.

Faster than any Buckingham ever, he charged the river bank and puffed into camp. He almost wept with relief when he saw that his own beast was still saddled. Upon his arrival, he'd taken time only to loosen its cinch and then had promptly forgotten about it.

For one pleading moment, he hung suspended between his desire for haste and the neatly folded clothing he'd forgotten which he could see resting in wait. The thought of racing across the prairie, wet and as bald and alabaster as an egg shell was the most abhorrent thing imaginable. Yet, what choice did he have? Even now, the shooting seemed almost upon him.

Darby turned resolutely away from his clothes. He quickly led the horses to a suitable fallen tree and stepped up to mount just as Pony Bob burst into the clearing with the Indians in full chase.

Darby's horse stampeded and he leapt across its back, draped like a giant sausage.

"Whoa. Damn you. Whoa!"

Valiantly, he strove to hang on while his face and that of his spare horse pounded up and down just inches apart. But at least his rifle was in the saddle boot and, as near as he could tell, the horses were running for Carson City.

"Sit up," Pony Bob swore, reining in beside and leaping onto the bare back of the lead horse.

"I'm trying!"

Pony Bob jerked the mochila free and his weary mount fell back. Then, the Express rider somehow pulled Darby erect. But none too soon. For the first time in his life, Darby knew the whirring sound of an arrow flying by his ear.

They tore out of the river basin into saged hills and the wild Indian whooping seemed ever louder.

"Use your rifle, Mr. Buckingham. I'm out of ammunition."

Darby didn't see how he could possibly fire a weapon. One hand was holding the reins and the other strangled his saddlehorn. He dared to glance aside and saw that Pony Bob was reloading with his reins clenched between his teeth. Darby saw an arrow glide by and decided he had to do something.

He bit the reins and yanked the Winchester free and levered it to fire. Problem was, he couldn't turn around. Try as he might, it was impossible to shoot over his shoulder on the running horse.

"Fire! Fire!"

Darby reversed the Winchester and pulled the trigger. He didn't even pretend to look back. He couldn't have if he'd wanted to. His intention was merely to keep them at a distance. When his third bullet singed the rump of his own horse, the animal took leave of the ground and its senses.

Darby grabbed for leather. He wasn't sure which would be worse—riding into Carson City like a plucked goose or having the Paiutes catch him. But it wasn't his decision. Their horses were rested and chosen solely for speed.

Even now, the hail of arrows had evaporated and the fierce yells were fading in the distance. They were going to make it.

May 23, 1860 NOTES: I must complete these thoughts now because tomorrow I ride north to battle the great Chief Numaga with a strong military force of over seven hundred. Surely he must be defeated this time, as we are well prepared and even dragging twelve-pound mountain howitzers. I fear there will be no quarter given, as the final account of the dead of Major Ormsby's ill-fated campaign is now forty-six. Most still lie somewhere out in the desert waiting for burial.

Eleven days ago, I was subjected to the most humiliating entrance ever to befall man. Yet, though bruised of pride and flesh, I was fortunate and consider it worthwhile and historic. I was instrumental in saving Mr. Pony Bob Haslam from death and participating in the longest ride in the annals of western history. Here is the true account of it as related by Mr. Haslam. The courage and drama of this man's simple narrative need no elaborations of my writing style.

'On May 11, I began my ride as usual from Friday's Station beside the Sierras. I had no idea what trouble awaited to the east and felt badly that I could not join the brave volunteers to march under Major Ormsby. Soon, however, I had my own Indian troubles.

'At my first station in Carson City, I discovered Ormsby's volunteers had commandeered all our horses sometime during the night before. There being no choice, I was forced to ride my tired horse clear to Fort Churchill. This was bad because, if the Indians had jumped me, my pony would not have been able to outrun them.

"At Fort Churchill, my relief rider, Billy Richardson, was very upset about the Indians and refused to carry the mail on to the next home station at Smith's Creek, 115 miles east. The station tender grew angry and offered me a fifty dollar bonus if I would take Billy's run. I accepted the challenge though I would have without the fifty.

'But at least I now had a fresh horse and was determined to make up lost time. Every hour that passed I expected a fight, but the Indians did not appear. After changing mounts at Sand Springs and Cold Spring, I finally reached Smith's Creek early on the morning of May 12. I was very tired, having ridden 190 miles in about 18 hours.

"At Smith's Creek, I handed the mail to Jay Kelly and warned him of the danger. Then I slept for eight hours until the westbound mail arrived for me to carry on. The sleep put me back in good shape and my horse was rested. I prayed the return would be fast and without Indians to fight.

'But, back in Cold Spring, my luck ran out. The station had been attacked by Paiutes and burned to the ground. The tender was shot full of arrows and our ponies were stolen. I was deeply worried. Once more, I was on a tired horse, and I believed the Indians were just ahead, lying in ambush.

'At Sand Springs, I found the stock tender waiting with fresh mounts. He was very scared when I told him about what happened at the last station. Maybe I shouldn't have, but I took the kid along with me because I was sure he would be killed if he stayed behind.

'I left the boy at Carson Sink with several well-armed

station men and pushed on toward Carson City. I was very
tired and my eyes kept closing as I wanted rest.

'Just before reaching the burnt-out remains of Williams
Station, they finally jumped me. My horse was done in, and
I thought sure I would be killed. Would have, too, if it
hadn't been for Mr. Darby Buckingham.

'I couldn't believe my eyes when he broke out of the
cottonwoods, wearing almost no clothes and flopping across
his saddle. But he hung on and with the fresh horses we
outran the Paiutes. Mr. Buckingham saved my bacon and
that is for certain.

'I felt like celebrating when we finally reached Carson
City on May 13. But my happiness went sour when I
heard about Major Ormsby and the forty-six dead. Everyone was real scared and thought for sure the Indians were
fixing to overrun the territory.

'I do not know if they will. I felt lucky to be alive and
pushed on to finish my ride at Friday's Station where Warren Upson took the mail over the Sierras to California. I
was so tired and wrung out I went to bed. I'd ridden across
380 miles of tough country and been worried about being
killed by Paiutes for the past thirty-six hours.

'If Indians attacked us at Friday's Station, I told the
station tender to wake me up for the fight.

                                    —Pony Bob Haslam, Express Rider

Darby placed his pen down and reread his notes.
Then, with a sigh, he closed the notebook, feeling very
proud to have been, in a very minor and certainly bun-
gling way, a participant in such a courageous slice of
history.

Yet, his mood was not light and his thoughts were
troubled. Tomorrow, he would leave with the military
expedition going to the Paiute stronghold. More lives
would be wasted and the future of the Pony Express
was severely threatened.

Even should Numaga be defeated, Bolivar Roberts
and others shared the firm conviction that the great
chief would never allow his tribe to be annihilated. If
the battle seemed lost, Numaga would retreat into the
northern mountains where the military and its cannon
would never be able to dislodge his warriors. And

shortly afterward, he would begin to raid the territory. Within that territory, the Pony Express, with its scattered and poorly manned stations, would be as vulnerable as an exposed artery.

In the end, the dream of Russell, Majors, and Waddell to capture the Overland Mail Route would go up in the smoke of their charred stations. The people who had called Pyramid Lake their hunting grounds for untold centuries would be forced into extinction, to die in a hostile, starving land.

"Blast!" Darby swore. Perhaps he could have come to grips with this great tragedy had it not been for the knowledge that he'd failed to convince those prospectors they *had* to be witnesses.

All seemed lost. It was possible that Evans and Brown might even have been killed by the same raiding party that chased Pony Bob. If so, there was nothing he could do to change the course of future events. It was, he thought bitterly, a terrible shame.

Darby packed his notes and writing materials into his bag. He would record this great folly. There seemed to be no choice.

Chapter 8

He was pouring a glass of brandy, his last on this troubled day, when the knock sounded at his door. More than likely, it would be Bolivar Roberts, trying one final time to dissuade him from riding north in the morning. It would have been easy for Darby to remain in Carson City, but he couldn't. Someday very soon, he intended to ensure that the true story behind the Pony Express War went on record—that meant he'd have to witness this final chapter.

"Buckingham. Open up. Quick!"

Darby set his brandy down hard and wheeled for the door. It wasn't Bolivar Roberts. He could have recognized that gravelly voice anywhere as belonging to Rollie Evans.

The old prospector was alone in the hallway and, as soon as the door opened, he squeezed in as though the devil himself had been courting his footsteps.

Evans swallowed noisily. "Got anything to drink?"

"Certainly, but . . ."

"Give it to me, Derby Man. I'll explain later."

He nodded and started to pour, but Evans snatched the entire bottle from his hands and upended it noisily.

He smacked his lips and color flushed his cheeks. "Damn, that was good."

"Glad you approve," Darby said. "Now, if you're ready to state your business, I'd be grateful. There isn't much time. The Washoe Regiment is starting for Pyramid Lake in the morning. Have you decided to talk?"

Rollie Evans emptied the bottle and Darby made no attempt to stop him. The last thing he could afford was to anger the old miner.

Rollie's eyes were moist and his voice raw. He winked and said, "You know, I barely got out of them hills alive when you and Haslam brought those Paiutes through."

"I was worried about you."

"The hell you were! Me and Hank know what you want. You've made no secret about it."

Darby almost bit his Cuban cigar in two. But he held his temper. Besides, there was truth in Rollie's words.

"I'm glad you escaped."

"Humph!"

"Did your partner fare as well?"

Evans glared at him. "Yeah, Hank is alive." The miner's eyes drew down to slits. "But he don't know I'm here. He would have none of it but, then, he never could see a gift horse when it came round the bend."

"Gift horse?" Darby frowned. "What do you mean?"

"I mean you smell like money," Rollie said bluntly.

Darby's mustache bristled. "So, you want me to pay you for telling the truth to the authorities. Is that right?"

"Yep."

Darby wanted to hit the prospector. Choke the truth out of him. He was so angry his voice shook with pent-up fury. "You've got the chance of stopping an Indian war. Do you have no conscience? No honor?"

Evans looked away. He scrubbed his whiskered face. "We lost everything out by Williams Station. Wouldn't have happened if that damned pony rider hadn't brung those Indians in behind. We left all we owned and now it ain't even safe to go back."

"How much do you want?"

"I don't like the taste of this any better than you do," Evans complained.

"How much?" Darby gritted.

"Plenty. Enough to get me and Hank out of this territory and to live on in California. If we talk, this country ain't going to be healthy for either of us."

"Damnit! How much?"

"I don't know," he admitted. "I thought by now you'd be beating the hell out of me for even suggesting it. You got any more of that brandy?" he asked suddenly.

"No. Now, you . . ."

Evans retreated for the door and Darby froze. The washed-out prospector cleared his throat. "What I seen shouldn't oughta been seen. I don't even like to think about it, Derby Man. So get me another bottle if you want me to talk. And . . . and when you get back, I'll be fixed on a price."

"Then what?"

"You're the writer," Evans said, his voice brittle as cracking brush. "I'll tell my story and you write it down."

"It would be better if *you* did," Darby said cautiously. "You could write it all out while I'm getting the brandy. I have some paper, ink and . . ."

"No!" Evans yelled. "The only thing I can spell is my own name. I'll sign what you write and then take the money and git."

"I'll need a witness," Darby said.

"Uh-uh. This is just between you and me."

"Then it's no deal." Darby watched the shock register and then pushed on. "Without a witness, I'd have no proof you signed it. I'd be wasting money."

Evans stared at him for a long time as though trying to decide if the writer was bluffing. "All right," he said with reluctance. "Who are you gonna bring?"

"Bolivar Roberts."

"Fair enough. But that's all."

"That's all," Darby echoed, pulling on his coat and starting to leave. "I'll be gone only half an hour at most."

As he was going out the door, Evans called, "Bolivar Roberts, the brandy, and lots of money. That's all I want to see. And don't tell anyone I'm waiting here."

Darby went down the hallway on the run. No matter what the price, it was a bargain. Fifteen minutes ago, there'd been no hope at all. Now, suddenly, the door had opened.

There was no time to lose.

Darby moved quickly. He'd dragged the Pony Express Superintendent out of his bed and pulled him into the street half dressed. Several more minutes were wasted at his favorite saloon procuring a fresh bottle of brandy. He was puffing noticeably when he assaulted the stairs and reached his door.

"Open up! It's me, Darby Buckingham."

There was no answer. The door was unlocked. He barged in and was in midstride when he saw Rollie Evans. The bottle slipped from his fingers and rolled across the scarred wooden floor.

"My God," Bolivar whispered. "He's dead!"

Darby trudged over to his bed and inspected the figure. Evans was stretched out with a gun clenched in one fist and a powder-burned pillow in the other. There was a sheet of Darby's writing paper on the bedside table.

"He killed himself," Bolivar said quietly.

Darby leaned over and peered down at the note, which read: "Buckingham. I'm a liar and a coward. I lived too long so now it's done."

No signature. Darby's eyes blurred. That was the only thing Evans could spell.

There had been two chances; now there was only one. Hank Brown would never talk and, in just a few short hours, the campaign against Numaga would begin.

Nothing could stop the battle to come. With the death of Rollie Evans, the opportunity was lost.

The Battle of Pinacle Mount was fought under the command of Colonel Jack Hays, a taciturn but shrewd leader who'd spent years fighting Indians in the Southwest. The Washoe Regiment he led boasted three surgeons, an acting adjutant of the infantry, quartermasters, a commissary officer, fifteen captains, and ten lieutenants. Altogether, their forces consisted of eight companies of infantry, and six of cavalry.

The civilians among them were a mixed lot, and Darby learned they marched and rode as Carson Rangers, Coloma Grays, Highland Rangers, Independent City Guards of Sacramento, Nevada Rifles, and a host of other titles.

They'd established a training camp the first night on a sagebrush flat near the Carson River, and they'd dubbed it Camp Hays in honor of their leader. Since departing from Carson City, a steady rain had fallen, and Darby could see the boisterous spirits of this army flagging noticeably. Yet, there were some, particularly the younger officers, who continued to brag of the great deeds they'd accomplish in battle. Darby thought this was a bad sign and, late that evening, as they sat huddled about their campfire, he quietly told Colonel Hays his feelings. For a moment, the tough old veteran fighter thought it over and then pulled Darby aside.

"You're right," he said. "I like officers who keep their mouths shut except when it comes to giving intelligent orders. And some of these young fellas need a lesson."

"How do you propose to give it?"

Hays scuffed the dirt, debated a moment, and said, "Stay back from the campfire and you'll see."

As Darby watched, just out of the ring of firelight, he saw Hays saunter in next to the campfire and bend close, as though seeking warmth. But he did something else. From his coat pocket, he slipped an unopened can of fruit into the ashes and then moved away.

Darby's interest quickened, and his eyes stayed glued to the hidden can. Nearby, Colonel Hays squatted down on a tarpaulin which covered his blankets, tugged his campaign hat low over his eyes to shield the rain, and observed his young officers carrying on their brag.

They didn't have long to wait. The can exploded like a mountain howitzer and showered the officers with burning coals and sparks.

"Injuns! Injuns!" their commander bellowed.

The effect was more than Darby could have hoped for. Most of the braggarts scattered wildly, running in every direction, some even through the fire itself. A couple were so stunned they were incapable of movement and just froze as easy targets, shivering with fear and indecision.

Of the lot, only a few were cool-headed enough to grab their rifles, jump for cover, and prepare for action. If it had been a real Indian attack, all the others would have been slaughtered like frightened rabbits.

Darby saw Hays mentally note those who hadn't panicked. The writer shook his head. In one stroke, their commander had discovered who his real leaders were, and he'd taught the rest a valuable lesson in humility.

Right there and then, Darby knew that Colonel Hays was going to whip the Paiutes. He had more than Ormsby's courage; he had a very calculating mind.

In the days to come, as they'd marched toward Pyramid Lake, Hays's intelligence and leadership steadied the men and brought them through several preliminary skirmishes. It also became obvious that Numaga was testing the strength of his adversary.

At Big Meadows, Colonel Hays's small advance force was attacked by Numaga's warriors, who attempted to lure them forward much like they'd done with Ormsby at Pyramid Lake. But Hays's orders had been to fall back for help and, this time, Numaga's trap clicked empty. A short battle ensued, but the warriors, failing to divide their opponent, wisely retreated with few losses.

Colonel Hays and the Washoe Regiment kept advancing, and Darby Buckingham filled his notebooks with impressions of the men, their growing confidence, and his musings and feelings about what would happen when they reached Pyramid Lake.

On the day before their arrival, Hays made an important decision to send a small unit of cavalry ahead to scout the lake and reconnoiter for Indians. Darby thought the selection of Captain Storey was another example of Hays's good judgment. He had already singled out Storey as one of their most capable leaders.

Edward Farris Storey was a man unlikely to wilt under fire and had once been a lieutenant in the Texas Rangers. Furthermore, he'd fought in the Mexican War and won distinction for his bravery at the Battle of Buena Vista. Afterward, he'd remained in Texas until his young wife died, and then he'd drifted through the Southwest, gaining experience fighting Indians. Captain Storey had seen more than his share of frontier action and was almost as respected as Colonel Hays himself.

The battle that followed and what happened to Captain Storey were neatly recorded by Darby Buckingham in an account which he read with a deep sense of regret.

Captain Storey and his detachment of cavalry were the first to see the lake. He told me later that he was surprised at the beauty of this vast body of water and remembered that the great triangular rock along the eastern shore, rising to a conical peak, had once given John C. Fremont the inspiration to name it Pyramid Lake.

He recalled also that the surface had been serene and tranquil, with wind-sculpted rocks jutting out of the gray blue, reflecting waters. There were thousands of birds skimming over the lake in search of food. Pelicans, inland seagulls, wild ducks calling, their voices echoing far across that great expanse of water. It had seemed impossible that death might await on that peaceful day.

As he'd approached what seemed to be a deserted Paiute camp, the Indians had swept out of their wooden karnee huts and attacked. Storey held his position until he saw a large band of mounted warriors pour out from a hidden gulley at his rear flank.

The men retreated up the same slippery trail upon which Ormsby had died. Storey and some of the others covered the retreat as best they could. Yet, their position was indefensible. More than three hundred warriors came at them on horseback in the form of an arrow head while as many others ran on foot.

At the very last moment, Storey and his defenders whirled and raced up the trail to regroup on the plateau above. Their losses were small but, just as before, the chase was on.

This time, however, Colonel Hays and the main body of our forces were waiting at the rescue.

I was there to see Captain Storey and his cavalry in full retreat and, unaccustomed as I am to fighting Indians, I admit my apprehension. Fortunately, Colonel Hays had no such thoughts. He coolly appraised Storey's desperate circumstances and gave his orders. He would rescue Storey, wheel and fight. Captain Stewart and the infantry would move in a wide advancing line across the plateau to sweep away all the Indians who were firing from hiding positions in the gullies and rocks.

Other officers were to guard the flanks and Captain Flint was to take an elevated position for the mountain howitzers.

All of this was ordered in less than half a minute. Then, we charged forward to rescue Captain Storey. When we met, Hays gave the order to dismount and we formed a walking line of riflemen. Under our heavy fire, Numaga and his pursuing warriors turned and fell back.

It was a wretched sight. Men on both sides were dying. I could hear the cries of the wounded and Colonel Hays shouting to go forward. To our right was Pinnacle Mount, and Numaga had stationed his best marksmen there. They fired down on us with devastating accuracy and our numbers thinned.

Captain Storey and his men were sent to take Pinnacle Mount, and I could not resist watching as they battled up that long and soon to be bloodsoaked peak. Numaga was on that mount and he fought and yelled, urging his warriors. Later, when the Indians finally were driven off by Captain Storey's men, the hillside was strewn with the dead.

My impression, in those swirling, terrible hours, was one of . . . how shall I put it . . . a strange combination of pride and pity. Pride for the courageous way both the Indians and our own forces battled so gallantly. And pity for the waste of their gallantry—that it should have to be.

Later, we discovered that Captain Storey had taken a bullet in the chest which perforated his lung and rendered him paralyzed. One of his men raced through gunfire all the way to the Carson River to get his leader a hatful of water; another knelt at his side, openly weeping and protecting Storey's face from the sun.

But, I saw another man come rushing up to the fallen Captain, wave a bloody scalp before Storey's face and yell, "Look, Captain, look! I killed the Indian who shot you!"

Storey, frothy lips bubbling with each gasp for air, cried, "Take it away."

When I saw that scalp, I confess to you, my readers, something inside me snapped, and I struck the soldier as viciously as anyone has even been hit. He fell without a noise and, for some reason, I picked up the scalp and took it away for burial. This I scarcely remember, as I was not of clear mind.

Later, it became apparent to all of us that the battle was

over. We had, or rather the now deceased Captain Storey had, broken the Paiute forces on Pinnacle Mount and Colonel Hays had eliminated all opposition across the plateau.

Numaga was almost the last wrrior we saw. On the crest of a hillside, he was bent low over the neck of his horse. I do not know if he was wounded or not. But he looked down upon defeat, and my own divided sympathies made my heart go out to him.

We'd won, driven his people from their land to God knows where. There was no celebration among any of us as we counted our dead and wounded. Even the young officers who'd been so brash at Camp Hays a few days earlier now seemed quiet and thoughtful.

The battle was over. Numaga was gone. Where, I asked, was the victory when both sides had suffered their dead?

Darby stopped reading and poured himself a brandy as he puffed on a fresh Cuban cigar.

A loud knock sounded at his door and it was Bolivar Roberts. The man saw Darby's notes and said, "Don't let it keep eating at you. It's over."

When Darby remained silent, he frowned. "Besides, we've got our own troubles. Think you can come with me back to the office?"

"Surely," Darby answered, downing his brandy and feeling glad to leave. "What's wrong?"

"You'll see. Mr. Finney is here."

At the Pony Express office, William F. Finney was scowling. "Unless we get help, the Pony is finished. I've . . . I've decided to cancel the June first trip."

"What!" Darby cried, "you've halted the Pony Express?"

Finney glanced over at Bolivar. "You didn't tell him?"

"I was going to. Guess I forgot."

Darby felt a great sense of defeat well up inside. "I didn't realize it was that bad," he said morosely.

"Oh, but it is. Just last night, I received word that the Indians have pretty well wiped out our smallest stations. Burned most to the ground and taken the stock. I . . . I don't even know how many employees are alive out there," he said.

"Something must be done," Darby said tightly.

"What? I've asked General Clarke over in California for aid. Told him we needed at least seventy-five soldiers to be posted at our relays between Sand Spings and Dry Creek. He regretfully declined."

"But why?"

Finney shrugged. "It's not his fault. He knows we're under siege out there. But he's already sent 150 men to stay with Colonel Hays, and he can't spare any more."

"Then we're whipped, aren't we?" Bolivar whispered.

Finney looked up. "Looks that way. As you know, the firm is under heavy financial pressure. Russell, Majors, and Waddell are fighting for government support but getting nowhere. Finances are in a bad way and to restock and rebuild our stations will cost plenty, to say nothing of rehiring those who quit or replacements for those who were killed in the latest raids."

Darby smacked his hands together. "It would seem to me, gentlemen, that it is time to plead our case with the people of California."

"What do you mean?"

"I mean," Darby told them, "since the very beginning of this gamble, the Pony Express has been taking a loss on every piece of mail it has handled. True, it is doing it with the purpose of eventually recouping its losses. But the fact remains that the main beneficiaries to date have been the people of San Francisco and Sacramento. I think it's time to call in the score."

Finney blinked. "You mean, raise our rates to reflect the true cost? They'd never stand for that, not all at once. Besides, if the Pony Express is inoperative now, that wouldn't help."

"True!" Darby said with a gleam in his eye. "So we throw ourselves on their mercy and generosity."

"But . . ."

"Look," Darby said, his words tumbling ever faster, "I'll compose a letter to be sent by telegraph. You decide to whom it should go. Someone, of course, who is powerful and influential enough to plead our case before the people. Let's tell them what we need and let *them* decide. After all, what do we have to lose?"

"Not a damn thing," Finney shouted, the beaten

look disappearing from his face. "Writer, get your quill and paper!"

Will California help the Pony in its difficulty? We have conferred some benefits, have asked but little, and perhaps the people will assist. Can anything be done in your cities toward paying expenses to furnish arms and provisions for twenty-five men to go through with me to Salt Lake City to take and bring on the Express mail?

I will be responsible for the return of the arms, will have transportation of my own and can find men here. What is wanted is $1,000 for the pay of the men, $500 for provisions, and twenty Sharpe's rifles, and as many dragoon pistols.

I will guarantee to keep the Pony alive a while longer.

Wm. W. Finney

For almost two weeks, Darby, William Finney, and Bolivar Roberts waited with growing anxiety. Meanwhile, the Pony Express was dead, for all intents and purposes. No mail traveled east or west. No white men crossed the great Nevada desert—only scattered bands of Numaga's warriors.

Finally, the telegraph began to click. Word from Sacramento *and* San Francisco sang out the message —CALIFORNIA WOULD HELP. Over twelve hundred dollars from Sacramento and that much again from San Francisco. And yes, the Sharpe's rifles and dragoon pistols would be sent immediately.

"I'll start hiring men today," Bolivar said with a grin.

Finney nodded. "Men who are seasoned fighters are the kind you need. Pick them well, or you might end up like Major Ormsby."

"Don't worry. I know who can shoot straight in this town."

"I'm not one of them," Darby said, "but, all the same, I'd like to go along."

"I'd be hurt if you didn't," the superintendent added, "but I know how much you hate a saddle and this will be a long trip."

Darby nodded. "I've ridden your fastest horses blind in the night and almost naked in the light of day. I'll make it. There's just one thing I regret."

"What's that?"

"I didn't find Hank Brown or Claude Tulley."

"Forget about them," Bolivar said wearily. "There's a good chance that Brown is dead. If he's still alive, he'll be hiding."

"What about Tulley? We can't just let him get away with murder."

"Do we have any choice?" Bolivar asked pointedly. "We both know he killed Rollie Evans, but we haven't a single shred of proof."

"Proof!" Darby raged. "I'm tired of needing proof. For the lack of it, a war that never should have started is taking place."

"Take it easy," Finney advised. "What's done is done. All we can do now is try and get the Pony Express back and running."

Darby's lips tightened and the muscles in his face were rigid. Never in his life had he felt so thwarted. Clayton was dead, and good riddance. But, as long as Tulley was free, justice had not been served.

"All right," he said after a long pause. "I agree the Pony Express is more important. We'll get it started again. But when that's done, I'm going to be leaving you for a while."

"To do what?" Bolivar looked worried. "Darby, if . . ."

"Please," Darby said, "I've grown to consider you men my friends. But don't make the error of thinking I work for you. I don't. And if I choose to step aside and concentrate my efforts toward seeing that justice is done, then that is my right."

"It is also *my* right, as your friend, to try to talk some sense into your head," Bolivar said passionately. He glanced at Finney for support.

"He's correct, Darby. If you go looking for Claude Tulley, only two things can happen. One, and the most likely, is that he'll kill you. You're not a gunman."

"And the second?" Darby rasped.

"The second is that you might somehow kill Tulley

but either hang or go to prison. After all, you'd be the one who provoked the shooting. And to beat Tulley, you'd have to get the drop on him."

Darby slumped. They were right. But so was he. "Then I've just one alternative. Somehow, I've got to find Hank Brown and make him testify."

"You'll never find the man," Bolivar said flatly.

"That's where you're wrong. I'll find him. If I have to crawl into every mine on the Comstock or hunt every back street in Sacramento or San Francisco, I *will* find him. And this time, I won't take no for an answer."

So saying, he bulled his way out of the office and headed down the street. It was late in the evening and he was too angry to go back to his hotel room. He wished that he and Bolivar were leaving tonight. At least they'd be *doing* something.

As he trudged along the street, Darby realized that the past two weeks had been among the worst in his life. At first, it had been one report after another about the Indian raids to the east. Stock tenders, stationmasters, and the Pony Express riders alike were abandoning their posts and fleeing to safety. No one blamed them. Numaga and his warriors, unable to overcome the superior military force, had adopted hit-and-run tactics, as expected. Station by station, they were going to wipe the Pony Express from the pages of history, and there wasn't a damned thing anyone, including Colonel Hays, could do to stop them.

It was true, Darby thought, the telegram from California did provide some hope. Yet, even if they did manage to reopen those ravaged stations, how long would they be in operation before the Paiutes returned?

These were his troubled thoughts as the writer plodded along, and so engrossed was Darby in their complexities that he didn't notice the man who'd emerged from the alley to confront him.

"Mr. Buckingham?"

He looked up suddenly. "Yes?"

"I got a message."

Darby didn't like the appearance of the intruder. He

was unkept and wouldn't meet his eye. Definitely not to be trusted. He decided to go on and ignore the fellow.

"Buckingham!"

The urgency was enough to make him stop and turn. "What's the message?" he asked shortly.

"Hank Brown wants to talk."

A jolt of expectancy and wild hope surged through him. Maybe, just maybe, there was a chance after all.

Chapter 9

"Where is he?" Darby cried.

The man displayed rotting teeth in a crooked leer. "Well now," he crowed, "it seems I got your attention, don't it?"

"You'll have more of it than you desire if you don't answer my question," Darby growled. "Now, where is he?"

"He's hiding, of course. Wouldn't you be if Claude Tulley was fixin' to nail your hide to the wall?"

"So, he understands what really happened to Rollie Evans." Darby's eyes narrowed. "If he's so worried, why isn't he running?"

"Money," the stranger said flatly. "It's easy enough to see you've got it. Hank wants some for traveling."

"And you?"

"Everybody needs money, don't they? I'm going to earn a few bucks for less than an hour's work."

"Where is he? I'm not paying anything until I get my . . . until I see him."

"Sure, sure. Hank says three hundred dollars will get him a stake in California. You carrying that much?"

"No, but I can have it in a few minutes."

"Then you'd better get it quick. Hank is taking a big chance and he's techy as a teased snake."

Darby nodded. If the man was nervous now, he was in for a whole lot worse until he decided to relate the story of Williams Station to the authorities.

"My room is just down the street," Darby said. "Wait here until I come back with the payment."

"If you want anything in writing, you'd better bring an extra two hundred," the messenger added quickly. "Five hundred, all together."

"You despicable vulture," Darby growled, "Hank

Brown will never see that extra two hundred, will he?"

The man backed away, realizing he was pushing his luck. "Take it or leave it, Mister."

"Stay here. I'll be right back."

As he turned away, the man called, "What are you so mad about? Famous writer and all. You got *plenty* of money. Everybody in Carson City knows that. Maybe even as much as Majors, Russell, and Waddell themselves. Five hundred is cheap!"

"Silence," Darby roared, pivoting.

The man held up his hands. "No offense. No offense, Mr. Buckingham. I was just repeating what people have said."

"Gossiping fools," he muttered, turning his back again and heading for his room.

Darby unlocked the door and put a match to his lamp. Then, he went to his closet and began pulling hundred dollar bills out of the spacious toes of his black shoes. It seemed a safe enough place to conceal his money. No western man would be caught dead wearing the black, round-toed city footwear he preferred.

He was in a hurry. The waiting was almost over. With luck, he just might be able to convince Colonel Hays and the military to negotiate an immediate truce. Perhaps the colonel would even accompany them, in hopes of meeting some of Numaga's warriors and initiating the first steps toward peace.

By heavens, that would be something! A real breakthrough. Sometimes a thing happened that suddenly made everything possible in a far easier way than one expected.

Darby halted in leaving. He gripped the doorknob and checked his impulse to rush down into the street. Beware the easy, the simple, the expedient. Occasionally, it did work, but more often it was trickery or illusion.

On the surface, the story he'd just heard seemed entirely plausible. Hank Brown would be fearful and in desperate need of money. After all, hadn't his partner said they'd been forced to abandon everything to escape the Paiutes? Yes. So he would need another stake, and it seemed entirely likely he'd want to go to California. Hank was a prospector and, although the forty-niner gold rush had long since been eclipsed by the new Comstock discoveries, there was still a fair amount of mining activity along the western Sierras. A man like Hank Brown probably had few alternatives for earning a living, and prospectors weren't known for liking cities.

Still, because it *was* so unexpected and almost too good to believe, Darby reentered his room and found a pepperbox pistol he'd bought only the week before. He now wished that he'd taken the chance to practice with the ugly little thing. But it was properly loaded and, in tight spaces, was capable of more than compensating for his own lack of marksmanship.

Darby tucked the squatty weapon into his waistband and pulled his coat over it. He glanced at the mirror and felt satisfied. On a thin man, the gun's shape would protrude most noticeably. But on his frame, the weapon was entirely inconspicuous. One more advantage to being on the robust side.

"It's about time," the man complained. "Another minute and I'd be gone. You get it?"

Darby patted the hidden gun. In his coat pocket, the five hundred dollars lay folded over his heart. If everything was as promised, he'd be more than willing to give them the cash. But, if not . . .

"Follow me."

"Where are we going? Do I have to ride?"

"No. Hank is hiding down in an alley."

Darby's first reaction was one of relief that he needn't clamber aboard a horse and that he'd confront the prospector at once. But his second reaction was entirely opposite. He wasn't accustomed to going into alleys. And how could anything proper be written in an alley?

"Blast," he swore, coming to an abrupt halt.

"What's the matter?"

"I forgot writing materials."

That threw the stranger off balance. He visibly grappled for his next words. "Well, ah . . . Hank's got some writing. Yeah, he already wrote it all out nice and proper." The self-satisfied smile was mocking.

"I see. Then you must have been pretty sure I'd come and bring the five hundred dollars," Darby said quietly.

"Just a little farther," the stranger answered. "If we don't talk so much, we could move faster."

Darby's hand brushed over the hidden pepperbox. With each stride, the conviction grew that he was being set up for murder. They traveled deeper into the shabbier section of town. Though a fresh and pleasant breeze was drifting off the Sierras, Darby felt the perspiration begin to flow.

"How much farther?"

"Just another block. You didn't expect Hank to go into the main part of Carson where someone might recognize him, did you?"

Darby said nothing. They'd walked to the north of the town, then cut west. Most of the houses were no more than shacks. Dogs barked; here and there, babies cried.

"This is it. Right on down the alley."

"I don't see him."

"I told you he was hiding."

"Tell him to come out."

"He won't do it. The man is scared."

Darby hesitated. Every instinct told him to leave at once. But the desperate need to find Hank Brown was irresistible.

The alley was as black as the inside of a well. He couldn't even distinguish whether it was blocked or open at the opposite end.

"I'll follow you," Darby said.

"Sure," the man replied after a short pause. "I know the way."

As soon as they entered, Darby reached down and gripped the pistol. It gave him some measure of confidence, but not a great deal. His eyes slowly grew accustomed to the darkness, and now he could identify shapes. Both sides were lined with shacks, and he saw piles of cans and an occasional rain barrel.

But no Hank Brown.

However, he did see that the alley opened at the far end and that made him feel better. If this was a trap, he'd at least have two avenues of escape. But . . .

Three feet behind him, a back door flew open and its hinges sounded like a knife blade going across rock.

Darby whirled and someone struck him with the force of a mule. He staggered and hands grabbed his coat and threw him against a board wall so hard that the breath shot from his lungs.

Fingers located his neck and bit into his skin. Darby brought a knee up hard and heard a grunt. The fingers spasmed and he tore them away and lashed out with all his strength. He missed. Swinging for a target one could not see was useless.

Darby closed against his opponent. It was like trying to grapple with a mountain. The man was huge and Darby knew without seeing that he was fighting Claude Tulley.

For a precious second, they strained, each trying to break the other. Darby locked his hands behind the taller man's back and began to squeeze while his opponent tried to force an arm around his neck. Darby didn't let him. His neck was short and as round as his thigh. In battle, it seemed to melt into his powerful shoulders and Darby kept his head buried under the man's chin.

"Ray, get him off me!" Tulley screamed. Darby planted his feet and pulled until he thought the sockets of his arms would separate.

"Ahhh! Ray, for . . ."

Ray hit him from behind with his gun butt. The blow missed Darby's head and caught him on the shoulder blade.

He felt something begin to crack in Tulley's spine and the man screeched. Ray struck again and Darby felt a numbness at the base of his neck that made his left arm weaken. Perhaps in five more seconds, he could have broken Tulley in half. But he didn't *have* five seconds. Ray wouldn't miss again. He might even be driven enough to shove his gun into Darby's back and pull the trigger.

Darby threw his weight to the side and let go. He

heard the sharp intake of breath and then gunfire begin to explode in the narrow confines of the alley.

Darby started to run. He could barely see, but he ran anyway. The alley rocked with gunfire.

Someone screamed and it was so high it couldn't have been Tulley. Darby crashed into a water barrel and spilled to the ground. He pulled his gun and, in a pool of dirty water, he elbowed down and began firing.

Again and again, he squeezed the trigger until all around him the alley rocked with explosions and smoke filled the air. When his gun was empty, he shifted sideways and waited. There was no sound.

"Claude Tulley, I know that was you. Come out with your hands up!" A bluff, true, but what other choice did he have? Silence stretched like piano wire until the tension vibrated.

"Tulley, are you hurt?"

He heard a low moan, then a whimpering sound like a boot being scraped across the ground. Darby crawled out of his mud puddle and inched forward. He kept thinking that if Hank Brown had already died and Claude Tulley was mortally wounded, there would never be a chance to prove his own suspicions.

Closer and closer he came, and realized he was pointing the empty gun toward the moaning sound. Somehow, it made him feel better and he kept pointing.

The moans were very close now and getting weaker as the seconds passed. Then, when he was no more than a yard or two away, Darby heard the death rattle.

"Tulley," he called.

It wasn't Claude Tulley. The man called Ray had breathed his last.

Darby stood alone. Tulley had vanished, leaving his fellow conspirator to gasp out his life in the filth of the alley.

His shoulders slumped as he realized he'd let the opportunity get away. Darby took a deep breath. "Blast!"

Then, he began to walk to town, absently flicking the mud from his suit with his fingernails.

They rode out of Carson City, twenty-five seasoned Indian fighters and Darby Buckingham. They took a large string of horses and a wagonload of supplies for rebuilding. New employees were to follow under William Finney when enough had been hired and the line reopened.

And they had to get it reopened soon, because Bolivar Roberts had more than a hundred letters which had piled up since the shutdown.

Darby was prepared for a hard ride, yet he didn't know how difficult it would be. It was the ninth of June and the weather had gone from snow and rain to heat. Heat that shimmered over the land and caused the salt-sting of perspiration to redden their eyes. And, at each station, they found a burned ruin, horses stolen and employees either dead or chased off.

Always, there was the threat of being ambushed. Bolivar Roberts kept riders out at the points, scouts ahead, and one man at least a mile behind to cover their trail. His thinking was that if the Paiutes did attack, their only chance would be to gather around the wagons and make a stand. And stand they would. These were not eager young men whom Bolivar had chosen. Rather, they were a stern lot, slow to speak, yet seemingly aware of everything and with the ability to communicate in gestures or with a look.

Riding among them, Darby felt almost as though he'd been transported back fifty years. These men were hunters; some spoke knowingly of traps and fur prices. Others, like Amos Teague, told of military battles and Indian fights. None bragged and those who spoke had a lean way with their words.

At night, they ate cold food and whispered together about people they'd known in "the old days." They spoke almost reverently of how it had been before the newcomers arrived. Not surprisingly, Darby was reminded of his two old friends back in Running Springs, Wyoming, Bear Timberly and Zack Woolsey. Buffalo hunters they'd been, and would be still if those days had not passed.

Darby missed his two old friends and knew they would love to be with him now, instead of trying to run their hotel and play at being respectable. There was another thing that bothered him—those two hellers would be trying to steal Dolly Beavers away from him. And, if he didn't send for her soon, they'd probably succeed.

That made him feel impatient to get back to Carson City. Maybe, when this Indian business cooled down and peace was finally restored, he *would* send for her. And, if she'd already grown tired of waiting and gone ahead and married Zack or Bear, well, there was no one to blame but himself. Dolly Beavers was too passionate a woman to spend her remaining years alone. Besides, she'd proposed to him at least a dozen times and he'd always refused.

He was caught in the dilemma which faces so many men. He wanted her, yet he needed his freedom too much to give it up, unless he was forced. And there *were* things about Dolly that drove him to distraction. That woman had a real talent for creating embarrassing moments. It didn't matter where she was. Without provocation or warning, she was as likely to throw a bear hug on a man as she was to slap his face if he so much as looked suggestively at her.

And she talked too much. Way too much and, no matter how often he'd told her, she still wore perfume strong enough to cause dogs and cats to run. Oh well, Darby thought, the woman did have her share of endearing qualities; most importantly, she loved him. The question was, did she love him enough to give him the freedom he needed to explore the West and write about it?

"Mr. Roberts," the rider called, galloping in from the north point. "I spotted Indians." All thoughts of Dolly Beavers vanished.

"How many?" the superintendent asked.

"Three."

"Paiutes?"

"I'm not sure."

Bolivar frowned. He leaned over toward Darby. "Probably a scouting party. If they're Paiutes, maybe we can talk them in. Set up a meeting with Numaga."

"And if they're not?" Darby asked cautiously.

"Then it's up to them. They might decide to hit us in the day if they've got enough warriors, or at night if they don't. We'd best push on to the Diamond Springs Station. It's made of rock and would be a good place to take a stand."

He turned to the scout. "Go on back, but keep a sharp eye. If you see more and they're gathering, you come in fast."

The scout might have been forty-five, or sixty-five. His face was deeply weather-lined, and his gray hair was long and moppish enough to cover his ears. Whatever his age, he was no fool. "Don't you worry. Ol' Jess ain't goin' to fall asleep out there. You'll hear me comin'."

They both watched him gallop away and Bolivar shook his head. "He'll be all right. But what about the new stations I'm supposed to build? I can't ask men to stay out in this country without protection."

Darby nodded. "The answer always comes out the same. We've *got* to reach Numaga and make a peace."

"Yeah, I know. But that ain't too easy. I gave him my word there'd be no trouble and look what happened."

"It wasn't your fault," Darby said, trying to make him feel better. "All we can do now is start over."

"I know. I know." He looked up. "One thing sure, I'll tell Finney that we need at least five men at every station this time until there's peace. And from now on, we're going to build our stations out of rocks or adobe. Build 'em like forts."

Darby kept his silence and watched to the north, expecting at any minute to see Jess come boiling out of the sagebrush with a passle of Indians right behind. But yet, Numaga might be among them and maybe . . . He brushed the thought away.

Two hours later, Jess came galloping over the hills. Darby felt his mouth go dry. It could mean only one thing.

"Mr. Roberts! There's more of 'em. At least thirty-five."

"How far?"

"Two, three miles out. But they're coming in a hurry."

Bolivar yanked his gun and fired twice to call in all

the scouts. "We're going to make a run for it," he shouted. "Diamond Springs is straight ahead. Teamsters, *move* these wagons. Let's go!"

There wasn't a man among them who needed to be told twice. In the still desert air, whips cracked like shot.

Darby grabbed leather and bent forward in the saddle. The faint trail of the Pony Express riders led to the east. No more than two feet wide, the track stretched off into the distance and vanished behind a hill. Darby couldn't see any rock fortress ahead. That didn't matter. He'd known Bolivar Roberts long enough to believe the man. Darby just prayed that the superintendent hadn't underestimated the distance to Diamond Springs, or that Jess hadn't misjudged how far off those Indians were.

A combined error of just one mile could be *very* fatal.

Chapter 10

They made it. In fact, Darby never did see the Indians. Jess was the only one who had and, after the stock was put up in a strong corral and the wagons grouped in the station yard, some of the men began to question old Jess's eyesight. That made him mad. He swore he'd seen Indians and offered to lead any of the skeptics out to find pony tracks.

His offer pretty well silenced the doubters. No one appeared eager to put his skepticism to the test.

Night fell quickly over the land and, as it did, the sagebrush began to assume lifelike qualities. Though hard men and seasoned, it was all Bolivar Roberts could do to prevent several of them from blasting away at what they believed to be Indians.

"Stay inside," Bolivar ordered. "Those of you who aren't on guard duty, keep down and try to get some rest."

Darby knew that wasn't going to be easy. The rock station was no more than fifteen or twenty feet square. And, like the other stations, it had been pillaged. The Indians had burned out the interior and the front door, yet the flames had only scorched the rock walls. They pushed out the charred debris as well as they could, but Darby still had the sensation of sleeping in a fireplace. The moment he lay down, the charcoal ashes filled his nose and everything he touched created a black smudge.

Yet, it was a fortress. There were even gun holes carefully mortised into the walls. Bolivar ordered boxes stacked chest high where the door had been. And, one by one, the men spread their blankets on the floor and bedded down for the night.

Guards would be spelled every two hours—three

men in the wagons, two by the corral, and another on the roof. Things appeared secure enough.

It was four in the morning when the last guard changed. One man groped into the room and hunted for the sleeping replacements.

And, while he was groping, the Indians attacked.

Darby had just been awakened for his turn. He was groggy still and upset because he'd lost one of his boots. In a way, he was very lucky, because the first man out took an arrow in the chest and died instantly.

The next sentry fared better. The arrow dug into the flesh under his arm and he made one hell of a sound. Fifteen men jolted by a blood-curdling scream, while packed tightly in their blankets, will create pandemonium.

The sentry who'd just shaken Darby awake bellowed into his face, "Indians! Indians!"

Darby managed to get out of his blankets. Someone ran into his back and went down hard.

"They're after our horses."

Gunfire began to pour across the yard as men streamed through the door. There was no thought of remaining within the sanctuary of those rock walls. Better to save the horses at all costs. They'd never survive a return on foot.

Darby, one boot on and one off, crow-hopped through the doorway, almost tripping over the body of someone. There was moonlight, but the gunfire was so heavy it seemed to give the station yard its own light.

"The horses. Get to the corral and help the sentries keep them away from our horses!"

Darby saw two Indians pounding across the yard. Shots blasted them down, but a hail of arrows lanced out from the sagebrush and then more warriors began to sweep through the yard on horseback. They came in death-dealing waves. Bent low on their ponies, they seemed to be a part of the wild-eyed animals. They were elusive targets, and many clung to the offside of their mounts and fired with either bows or rifles.

Darby was halfway between the stone house and the corral when he saw the unmistakable silhouette of Numaga. The chief disdained the cover of his horse's body. He sat upright with a war lance balanced in one hand and a rifle, which looked like a child's toy, in the other.

"Numaga!" Darby shouted.

The chief reined his mount in closer and then drew back his lance. He hesitated. Darby couldn't be sure if he did so out of recognition or merely to ensure his aim. But he *did* hesitate and that, plus his great size, made him an easy target.

A rifle slug struck his horse and the animal went down hard, pinning Numaga to the earth. Behind Darby, someone gave a blood-curdling yell and charged by toward the trapped Indian. It was Amos Teague! Amos, who'd bragged of taking scalps years ago in the Dakota country. Amos, with an Indian hatchet raised to strike.

Darby raced after him. He could see Numaga struggling to get his trapped leg free. Then, the chief saw Amos and desperately sought a weapon. The rifle he'd carried was gone—only the war lance remained.

Numaga grabbed for it, twisted in Teague's direction and braced himself to defend the charge. Yet, his circumstances were hopeless. The war lance was a good six feet long and almost impossible to manipulate from the ground.

Darby heard Numaga shout and saw him kick the lance up, balance it by the end and, incredibly, hurl it toward his attacker.

As unbelievable as the feat seemed, it was in vain. The throw lacked force and trajectory and the lance wobbled in the air.

Still, it made Amos Teague pitch headlong to the dirt to avoid being impaled. And that gave Darby the fraction of a second he needed to close distance on the old Indian fighter.

Teague climbed to his feet, threw back his tangled, gray mane and once again howled that blood-curdling, primeval cry. He raised the hatchet and Darby jumped for the old man's back. His shoulder drove into Teague just below the point of the ribs and his momentum carried them right over Numaga.

Darby landed on top of the Indian fighter and

chopped him once at the base of the skull. The man never knew what hit him.

"Numaga, it is I, Darby Buckingham."

The chief looked stunned. "Why did you do that?" he said in his clipped, perfectly taught missionary English.

"We want peace. I know about those young girls who were abused at Williams Station. So does Bolivar Roberts."

"You said our hungry would be fed by the Pony Express. You lied!"

"Those men were strangers. They killed our men and committed the outrage. I'm trying to prove this." Darby jammed his hands under the dead Indian pony. "Pull your leg out. Now!"

Darby lifted against the enormous weight. He sank to his knees and his thick back and arms knotted in a terrible strain. His neck appeared to dissolve into his round shoulders and, inch by inch, the carcass rose until Numaga rolled free.

The chief stood up, but the injured leg would not hold his weight. Maybe it was broken, perhaps only numbed. Either way, it didn't matter because Numaga was staring at Darby as though witnessing some mystery he could not fathom.

Behind them, the battle continued to rage, but the two powerful men didn't notice.

"You saved my life. I will spare you and the others. You have the strength of the great bear. Are you his brother in spirit?"

"No," Darby said, "just an ex-circus strongman. What about peace?"

Numaga glowered. "It is too late, Darby Buckingham. You must leave our lands. Go. While you are still alive!"

"But . . ."

Numaga cupped his hands to his mouth and shouted—twice—a loud, barking noise unlike anything Darby had ever heard. Then, his warriors split away from the battle and disappeared into the night. When Darby wheeled around, the Paiute chief was gone. Bad leg or not, it was as though he'd been swallowed by the land itself.

Darby picked up Amos Teague and carried him back to the station. Candles were lit and Bolivar Roberts called the role. They'd gotten off remarkably well—two men dead and three wounded, though none seriously. And they'd managed to prevent the Indians from running off their horses.

Amos Teague finally awoke and the first thing he wanted to know was if they'd scalped Numaga. When told the big chief had escaped, he swore a streak and wondered out loud what had fallen on him. Darby kept quiet. Maybe someone had seen him pull the horse off the Paiute chief, but he doubted it. The light had been poor and the action too fast-paced for anyone to have been concerned with anything but self-preservation. Besides, most of them had gone to fight out by the corral.

Darby was relieved. He was among Indian fighters and Indian haters. They wouldn't have accepted his motives. A good Indian was a dead one, and to hell with any extenuating circumstances.

But Numaga's hesitation when Darby called his name had been the mistake that led to his vulnerability, and the writer couldn't just let him be killed. And there was another thing he remembered, and that was the chief's final words, telling him to leave the Paiute lands while he was still alive. Not exactly a fond farewell, he thought bleakly.

Later that afternoon, Bolivar Roberts motioned him to ride off a ways. When they were out of hearing, Bolivar leaned over and said, "Well, are you going to tell me if you and the chief are blood brothers now?"

A rueful smile lifted the corners of Darby's mouth. "Not exactly," he confided. "Numaga told me to get out of his country—while I could."

"That's what I was afraid of." He pulled a bandanna out of his hip pocket and mopped sweat from under his hatband. "It's too late now for peace."

"If you really believe that," Darby said, "then we're wasting our time and the people of California's money by coming out here. We either make a truce or the Pony Express is finished."

Bolivar Roberts opened his mouth to speak but changed his mind and yanked his Stetson down low over his eyes. Without a sideways glance, he spurred away. The man knew Darby was right, but he'd lost all hope.

Darby shook his head in despair. Bolivar probably understood Numaga and the Paiutes as well as anyone. If the superintendent was resigned to a long and bloody campaign, what chance was there?

On the seventh day out of Carson City, they finally reached Roberts Station, more than 225 miles to the east. They met Superintendent Howard Egan and a U.S. detachment of troops under a Lieutenant Perkins.

"Bolivar, we've got some mail for you going west," Egan said.

"And I've more than a hundred for you."

"Ha." Egan laughed. "Your west coast folks are illiterate." Then he slung a bag at his counterpart which held over three hundred letters.

They didn't spend long at Roberts Creek, but there wasn't a man among them who wasn't glad to hear that Lieutenant Perkins and his soldiers were to escort them back to Carson City. It was the kind of news that made Darby feel a whole lot better.

The return trip was blissfully uneventful. Darby, feeling as though his stubby legs were going to be bowed for life, slipped off his horse in Carson City on the twenty-second of June. They'd been gone almost two weeks and ridden nearly five hundred miles. If that wasn't bad enough, Darby was appalled to discover he'd lost another ten pounds. It was sufficient to propel him in the direction of the best eatery in town.

The steak was roast sized, the potatoes steaming and laced with melted butter. An entire loaf of sliced bread lay before him and the waiter had found a particularly delicious apple jam. Darby was salivating with expectancy and his eyes were almost dreamy as his nose courted every nuance of aroma.

Then Bolivar Roberts hurtled through the front

door. "Darby," he panted, "take off the bib and let's get moving!"

The writer's mustache that, an instant before, had been quivering like a tuning fork as he surveyed his feast, now bristled.

"You're mad. Nothing could force me from this plate. Every fiber of my body cries for this sumptuous repast. I *must* eat before I waste away."

"Phooey. There's no time. I've just received word that as soon as we can guarantee the crossing, the mail will go on a *twice* a week schedule."

Darby shrugged and began to carve the red meat on his plate with as much attention as an artist might give to the movement of his brush or a sculptor to the chisel.

"Don't you understand," Bolivar ranted. "In spite of the greatest difficulty, at the very blackest hour, Majors, Russell, and Waddell have chosen to spit into the face of adversity."

Darby dusted the steak with pepper, then chose the most delectable morsel on his plate. His stomach rumbled happily.

Bolivar glowered fiercely. "Well, I thought you'd be pleased—even delighted. It means you can go on with your story. That's what you're here for, isn't it?"

"No, I'm here to eat. And, right now, I don't see what the big stir is about. Nothing has been solved regarding the Paiute trouble. Let me enjoy this banquet. Please."

"All right," Bolivar spluttered. "But first you should know that I had another piece of information and you can choke on it for all I care."

The meat hung tantalizingly close to his lips. "What is it?"

"I got word that Hank Brown is drunk and on a rampage up in Virginia City and that Claude Tulley went after him."

"Blast . . . Blast!" Darby screamed, dropping his fork into the mashed potatoes. "We've *got* to stop him."

"*You've* got to," Bolivar corrected. "I've not a minute to waste in revising my two-a-week schedule."

"Blast your schedule," Darby choked, rising to his feet and hurling his napkin into the food with disgust. "A man's life is in danger. The future of the Pony Express hangs in the balance."

Bolivar Roberts nodded. "I'm confident you are equal to the challenge," he said solemnly. "Let me know what happens."

Then, right before Darby's feverish eyes, the man pivoted on his boot heel and left.

Darby wanted to cry. Would it really matter if he waited only five minutes to eat? Dear Lord, would it?

The answer was self-evident—it might. Darby sighed as a man resigned to accept his responsibility. He dropped money on the table, then turned and trudged away, looking almost beaten and hearing his stomach growl.

At the door, he stopped and looked back. Then, his composure broke. He launched himself across the room, ripped off the napkin and took two big fistfuls of steak.

All the patrons stared in disbelief. Let them. If this had been his test to qualify as civilized and sophisticated, then he'd failed miserably.

Darby crammed one entire handful of steak into his maw. It was heavenly. With a greasy hand, he waved farewell and started for the livery.

So be it. He was a barbarian at heart.

Chapter 11

Darby Buckingham rode east along the broad, wagon-rutted pathway that led up to the already famous Comstock Lode. He passed high-sided ore wagons and mule teams pulling tons of supplies to the burgeoning cities in the hills beyond.

He'd been wanting to pay a visit to Virginia and Silver Cities from the day he'd arrived at the Pony Express office and met Bolivar Roberts. Carson City was no more than a stopover, really, for the great bonanza that lay under Sun Mountain only twenty miles east. And, during his stay, he'd listened eagerly to the fabulous tales of wealth discovered just beyond these rocky hills. Here, the great ore bodies rested deep underground instead of on the surface as they had in California. Every day, shafts were blasted deeper and deeper into the earth, and huge steam engines were being sent around the Horn and even from Europe to meet the frantic demand.

Yet, besides the vast discoveries which miners prophesied would never end, Darby had listened to other tales of the Comstock—fires in the mines, poison gases, and the terrible heat in the depths at which they worked. There was a purplish, claylike rock which defied shoring. When fresh air caused its mass to expand, a cave-in was the disastrous result.

Virginia City, Gold Hill, Silver City—only a couple of years old, they'd already earned the reputation of being hard places to live, and easy places to die.

Darby didn't need to ask directions. About five miles east of Carson City, the road angled north and began to ascend Gold Canyon. Freighting traffic was heavy and he saw giant processing mills with lines of creaking ore wagons patiently waiting their turn to be unloaded.

Everywhere Darby looked, he saw prospectors scouting the hills or busy at work. Red soil mounds dotted the hillsides, and the angry clanging of pick and shovel filled the air. To the writer, it seemed as though he'd entered some strange and foreign land. Up here, the landscape was bleak; no greenery contrasted the gray and mauve-colored hills. And no one spoke—only worked with a speed and intensity that defied description. The entire Comstock seemed to buzz with life and immediacy. Darby had the feeling that, as great as the ore bodies might be, these antlike workers were racing time.

He rode by several huge, wooden water tanks which were at least twenty feet high and as far across. Iron-ringed, they would supply Silver City with its life's blood during the hot months to come.

Later he passed over the steep Divide and let his winded horse blow while he gazed at Virginia City. Darby couldn't believe the size of it! Row after row of buildings along the main street and, for a mile both east and west, more than a thousand tents. Humanity crawled all over the hills and immense scaffolding works poked into the clear azure sky like broken winter trees.

Darby could have spent a long while at the Divide, but the very urgency of his mission made that impossible, so he urged his horse down into the central business district. He counted no less than thirty saloons along C Street and, above and below, there were other streets that looked equally busy. Unless he got very lucky, it might take him the entire day to locate Hank Brown—if Claude Tulley didn't find him first.

Thinking about Claude, the writer checked and made sure his pepperbox was loaded and ready. He had no illusions about being able to outdraw his opponent. But it was likely they'd meet in one of the crowded saloons. In that case, a pepperbox at short range was more than equal to a six-gun, if he could drag the cumbersome thing out of his coat pocket fast enough. He tied his animal at a hitch rail, pulled up his sagging trousers and entered the first saloon.

It took Darby three hard, tension-racked hours to

find Hank Brown. Hard, because his stomach knotted every time he entered another establishment, wondering if he'd meet Claude Tulley. He wasn't afraid of the confrontation; to the contrary, he saw it as inevitable but highly dangerous.

There was a score to settle and he meant to do it as soon as possible. Yet, Darby was a rational man and acknowledged the possibility that he could be killed. What made him want to avoid Tulley was the fact that he first had to locate the prospector and make him tell his story to the authorities. Afterward, the devil could decide the outcome but, either way, Claude Tulley was a dead man. If Darby failed, Tulley would be arrested, tried with rape and murder and sentenced to hang. That's why, when he saw Claude Tulley emerge on D Street from a saloon, Darby turned and ducked into hiding until the man was out of sight.

"Hey, Mister Darby Man, you lookin' for me?"

He whirled around. And there, swaying on his feet, was Hank Brown. He held a bottle in one hand and an old Navy Colt revolver in the other. It was the Colt that Darby watched. It was pointed right at Darby's stomach.

"Mr. Brown," he said, trying to keep his voice smooth and relaxed. "I've been searching for you all over Virginia City."

"So join the crowd. Everyone wants me dead. But," he said with a wink, "you sure as hell are in for a big surprise."

Darby felt the hair on the back of his neck start to prickle. Drunk or not, there was an unmistakable malice in the old prospector's voice.

"Get moving, Derby Man. Straight down those rows of tents until we get up in the country."

"What are you going to do?" he asked, knowing very well the nature of Brown's intentions.

"I'm sick of answering your questions! Just move or, so help me, I'll drop you right here in the street."

Darby believed him. Hank Brown was drunk enough to pull the trigger but sober enough to hit where he aimed.

The old man shoved his Colt into his waistband but

his hand didn't stray an inch from the gun butt. "Move! No, put your hands down. Act normal."

Act normal, Darby thought abysmally. How could anyone do that while he was being herded to the slaughter? He *had* to reason Brown out of this.

"Mind if I talk?"

"Sure as hell do. That's all you ever want to do is talk. Did you talk to my partner before you killed him?"

Darby spun around. "I didn't kill Mister Evans."

"Yore lying, Derby Man. He went to see you and that's the end of him."

"Claude Tulley must have killed him. The *Carson Appeal* said it looked like suicide, but . . ."

"Suicide. Rollie Evans never knew the damned word!" the prospector shouted. "He told me we should try and get you to pay our way out of this country, but I'd have no part of it. I thought he'd listened but, for the first time ever, he crossed me and went when I fell asleep."

"Evans didn't cross you," Darby said quietly. "He asked for five hundred dollars. Half of it was going to be yours."

The Colt sagged in the prospector's fist. "He . . . he said that?"

Brown needed to believe him and it was easy to tell the truth. "Yes. Your partner knew you'd be mad. And he knew the risks. He told me something else."

"What?" Hank Brown choked, upending the bottle of whiskey and wiping his eyes with a dirty shirtsleeve.

"He said he felt badly about the Indian trouble and was glad he was going to set the record straight."

Hank nodded. "Yeah, we talked about that aplenty. Rollie was a fool. If he'd used his head, he'd still be alive. His mistake was going to see you."

"No!" Darby roared. "*Your* mistake was not listening to Bolivar Roberts that first time we begged you to tell us what happened at Williams Station. If you'd done that, you'd both be working your claim and not worried about being scalped by Paiutes. None of this would have happened."

Brown staggered, his face contorted with anger and

grief. "It wasn't our fault," he cried. "All we wanted was to be left alone."

The two men stood facing each other. Right then and there, Darby decided he wasn't going another step out of Virginia City. If Hank Brown intended to kill him, he'd have to do it where someone was certain to be watching.

"Move."

"I'm not going anywhere," he said with conviction.

Hank cocked back the hammer. "You're going to hell in about one second unless you turn and walk."

Darby swallowed. The pepperbox sagged in his pocket, but he knew he'd never get it free in time.

"Claude Tulley killed your friend," he said as simply as he could. "If you kill me, he'll get off scott free. But, if I live, he'll hang. Is that what you want, your partner's murderer to go unpunished? *Even* after he kills you?" Darby asked, raising his eyebrows in question.

"No, but . . ."

"But nothing," Darby lashed. "Think, man! What would I have gained by killing your friend?"

He waited, saw the indecision and pressed hard. "Then ask yourself what Claude Tulley had to gain. Two questions, Mr. Brown. Ask them before you pull that trigger and make Tulley a free man."

Hank lowered the gun, then let it dangle harmlessly by his side. He'd asked, and the answers were loud and clear.

Darby reached into his pocket for a handkerchief to mop his clammy forehead. The danger was past and he felt almost weak with relief.

"So, what now?" Hank muttered. "Do we go looking for Claude Tulley? Maybe the two of us can take him, but don't count on it. He's supposed to be as good with his gun as he is with his fists and boots."

"No," Darby replied. "First you give me a drink out of that bottle and then we find Colonel Lander. I've heard he's out on patrol looking for a site to build a fort. We'll find the man and tell him everything."

"No dice, Mister! I want Claude Tulley."

"So do I. And I promise you we'll see him hang.

Wouldn't you rather have the man go that way than die fast with a bullet?"

"You bet I would."

The way he said it made Darby reach for the whiskey bottle and drink long and deep. "Then let's ride," he said, his throat burning fire from the cheap whiskey.

"I ain't got a horse."

"We'll find a stable and I'll buy you one. All I want to do is get out of here before Tulley sees us."

Evans nodded. "Don't worry, if he had, I'd be dead by now."

When Claude Tulley saw Darby Buckingham and Hank Brown rein east out of Gold Canyon, he almost laughed with relief. He stood and began to walk down toward his horse. If they had ridden west to Carson City, he'd have been forced to angle across country with very little time to prepare an ambush. But now . . . now, it was going to be so easy; every mile they traveled carried them further from civilization and made it more certain that there would be no witnesses.

Claude took his time. He absently tightened his cinch and tried to guess why the pair had gone east toward the desert. Perhaps, he thought, the dude had some harebrained idea of returning to burnt-out Williams Station and then having the old prospector re-enact the events.

Tulley scoffed. It would be a waste of time. There'd been snow and rain since the massacre that day. All tracks and evidence would be gone. Still, he knew Buckingham was a writer, and that made him an enigma, a man who couldn't be trusted to act predictably.

There was another, more likely, possibility that Tulley considered. Maybe the prospector and his sidekick had discovered a real find out near the Carson River. Perhaps the old devil had insisted on returning once more to his claim and packing out a stash of hidden gold. Tulley warmed to that idea. If it were so, he'd not only eliminate the two meddlers, but he'd also stand to gain a ripe nest egg.

And he could use one. He'd taken over Clayton's ranch and it had possibilities. Yet, without working capital, it could take him years to build it up into a paying operation. Tulley sucked in his breath and gathered his reins. Wouldn't this be his lucky day! With Clayton's spread and the prospector's gold, there was no telling what he could do. Down in the Carson valley, there were a lot of weak sisters ranching. They could easily be bought out or forced into deeding over their land. Tulley mounted and there was a serene and confident expression on his face. This could be his day.

He guided his horse down the rocky slope, taking care that he remained out of sight. There was no hurry and, if the two he followed saw him, he'd still be able to run them down and finish them off, but he'd never find the prospector's gold. Better to hang back and give them plenty of room; he could take them at sunset or sunrise. Take them as easy as knocking crows off a fence line.

Late that afternoon, Tulley realized his mistake. The old man and Darby Buckingham rode past Williams Station without even turning their heads.

Tulley cursed long and fervently. No hidden gold to bankroll those lofty plans he'd been making throughout the afternoon's quest. Gawdamnit, anyway! Where the hell *were* they going? Didn't the fools realize they were traveling deeper into Indian country? Every mile they rode increased the chances of being spotted by the cussed Paiutes.

The Indians made Tulley shiver. First the massacre below, where he'd been spared only by chance; then that nightmare up at Pyramid Lake under Major Ormsby. Twice he'd barely escaped being scalped. And now, here he was again pressing his luck. It made his stomach tighten. He had the feeling he'd pushed good fortune as much as he dared.

Claude spurred his horse across the Carson River and whipped it along a wide sandbar. He'd made his decision. Just as fast as he could, he was going to swing around in front of his quarry and blow them out of their saddles. They were less than a mile down river.

He could shoot them both, throw the bodies in the water and be on his return trip in less than an hour.

But he sure had been hoping for some gold. Maybe, he thought glumly, as his horse clattered over a rocky stretch, maybe this isn't going to be such a lucky day after all.

Chapter 12

Darby hadn't been idly enjoying his ride as they'd pushed on in search of Colonel Lander. In fact, he'd already wrung the entire story about Williams Station out of Hank Brown and had produced writing materials, from his saddlebags, scrawling the account as well as he could. It wasn't easy balancing a notepad across his saddle horn. Usually his script was bold and written with a flourish. Not this day.

He didn't care. It was in writing. They'd stopped long enough to allow Hank Brown to haltingly struggle over the words, nod his head that it was accurate, and sign the paper as being his own account of what had occurred at Williams Station, May 7, 1860.

Darby listened to the reading and decided he'd use it in his Pony Express story, just as Hank related it, without any literary embellishments.

"That does it," he said, folding the document and carefully placing it in his inside coat pocket.

Hank Brown scowled. "If that's all it takes, why don't you and me part company? I could ride back to our camp, collect a few things and be on my way."

"What about Claude Tulley?"

Hank glanced away. "I've been thinking about that. I'm sober now, but my head aches and I don't feel so good."

"You still want to see him hang, don't you?"

"Course I do! That's why I signed that paper." His pale, washed-out eyes snapped back to Darby. "But this ain't whiskey talking now, Derby Man, I . . . I didn't come hunting for you when I thought you was the fella who killed Rollie. No, I ran off to Virginia City and got drunk. That oughta say somethin'."

Darby pulled his horse to a standstill. "If you're trying to tell me you're a coward, Hank, I won't believe it. A coward wouldn't have signed the paper. Yes, you should have come forth and told the truth. It would have saved plenty of lives. But that's past."

"Look," Hank said, his voice desperate, "I'll fight for what's mine, but . . . but this ain't finished. And it won't be until Claude Tulley's neck stretches. Until then, I want out of this country. I'm ashamed to admit this, but I'm scared. I just want out."

Darby nodded. He didn't blame the old prospector. After all, the man had been living in fear of Tulley for weeks. It showed. But still, Darby wasn't certain that the document he'd written would stand up as evidence or convince Colonel Lander. It should, but could he bet everything on it?

"You place me in a dilemma," he said quietly. "There's a chance you'll have to testify in person."

"But why? Damnit, I signed my name. That oughta be enough."

"Should be," Darby admitted, "but I'm no lawyer. Tulley could swear you were lying. Or that this really wasn't your signature, or that I forced you to sign against your will."

"But that's not true!"

For a moment, they remained locked in silence. Finally, Darby shrugged. "Let's try it this way," he hedged. "I'll let you go if you promise to stay in one place where I can reach you. When we have Claude Tulley in jail, you could come over and testify if it be necessary."

"That sounds good to me," Hank said, his face coming alive. "Where do I hole up?"

Darby thought a minute. "Go to San Francisco. The man you want to see is William Finney. Tell him I sent you, then keep in contact."

"I'll do 'er! Yessir, I will. But . . ."

"What's wrong?"

"Well, I've been over there before. It's a rip-roaring town and it knows how to separate a man from his gold dust. It's been practicing since the rush of forty-nine."

"You need money. Is that the problem?"

"Well," he drawled, forcing a sheepish grin, "now that you mention it."

Darby yanked out his wallet. "Here's a hundred dollars. If you do as I've asked, you'll get another hundred when you come back to testify."

"Well, thank you! Real generous, Mr. Derby Man."

"Real important," Darby answered. "I'm writing a book on the Pony Express. I want to make very sure it ends satisfactorily. And, Mr. Brown, *you* are the key."

"You mean I'm going to be in your book?" The prospector's eyes danced.

"Of course. And if you keep your word from here on out, history will record you as being anything but a coward. What I'll write will make you proud. But . . . ," Darby's voice dropped, "but if you run out on us, I promise your name will be vilified."

"Vilified?" His busy eyebrows raised in concern. "That don't sound so good."

"It isn't. Don't make me do that."

The prospector nodded. "I won't. You got my promise, even without the money. I'll keep it." Then he stuck out his work-roughened hand and they shook.

"Good hunting, Derby Man."

"I'll see you in court," Darby called.

The old man waved back and there was a big smile on his face. And why not? He had a good horse, a new saddle, plenty of money and was riding toward a place in the history books. Everything was right.

Then—everything was wrong. Claude Tulley jumped out of cover, raised his Winchester and took deliberate aim. Darby heard the prospector's strangled cry of fear, saw him jerk upright in the saddle and try to rein his horse away.

They were a hundred yards off and Darby knew there was absolutely nothing he could do. The Winchester barked. Hank seemed to leap out of his stirrups. His arms flapped. Again, the Winchester thundered and Hank convulsed into a ball and pitched off his racing horse.

Darby wanted to shout with anger and despair. But, instead, he grabbed the pepperbox out of his coat and spurred forward. The horse leapt so abruptly he almost went over its haunches. Claude was afoot and Darby meant to run him into the ground. There were no witnesses left. It didn't matter. There would be no trial. With the death of Hank Brown, all of society's laws were cast aside in a single murderous rage for personal justice.

Darby extended his arm, aimed the pepperbox and began to pull the trigger. The stride of his horse was making his gun bounce up and down, but he didn't care.

The pepperbox fired again and again while smoke erupted. Through that cloud he saw Tulley lift the Winchester and take aim. Then, suddenly, the rifle splintered in his hands. Darby was amazed. He'd actually hit something with a pistol!

He fired twice more and the giant dropped his rifle and started running as horse and rider bore down on him. Darby's gun was empty. There seemed only one thing he could do, though he was certain it would result in a broken neck. He disentangled his foot from the off-stirrup, leaned toward the fleeing man and jumped.

But, even as he launched himself, he knew his timing was all wrong. He'd intended to land on Tulley's back. What was happening was that he was going to come up short. He'd been a split second early and, as he fell, he barely managed to throw out an arm in desperation and clip Tulley's boot.

Darby belly flopped into a sagebrush and the air exploded from his chest. He rolled and somehow came to his feet in time to see big Claude drag himself up to stand. Darby lowered his head and charged as Tulley grabbed for his Colt.

Darby connected first and as Tulley grunted his mouth flew open. Darby stepped back and kicked the man's fallen handgun away. For a moment, the two huge combatants just stood apart, trying to regain their breath. Both men were doubled at the waist, mouths open, nostrils flared. Yet, their eyes were locked across the few feet that separated them and Darby knew their long-awaited battle was about to get underway.

Very deliberately, he balled his flat, fighter's hands,

and his neck seemed to lower into his shoulders. They were contrasts in power—one tall, beautifully proportioned and muscular, the other all compact roundness but giving every indication of having his own immovable strength. The mountain lion and the wolverine. The mastiff and the pit bull.

Claude Tulley laughed as Darby began to rock from side to side. "You're a fool, Buckingham. You had six shots and all you did was ruin a good Winchester rifle. Now . . . now, I'm going to ruin you."

Darby jabbed but his opponent easily danced out of range. The man was like a cat on his feet. And Darby well remembered that those feet were Tulley's primary weapons.

"I killed your only witnesses," Tulley crowed. "Got 'em both and nothin' can touch me now."

Darby pounced forward and drove a left that thumped like a war drum into Tulley's ribs, but he had to take an overhand in return.

They backed off, Tulley leaning just a degree or two over his damaged side and Darby hearing a faint buzzing in his head from the punch.

"You put those arrows into our station keepers, didn't you?" the writer panted.

"Sure. But I made sure there were bullet holes first."

Darby charged and Tulley kicked him and dodged away in time to avoid the outstretched hands.

"You aren't going to get those arms around me again," Tulley gasped, dancing back.

The man's kick, taken in the front of his thigh, hurt like hell, but Darby tried not to show it as he watched Tulley begin to circle toward his gun. Darby cut him off. He planted his feet over the weapon and braced himself.

"You want your gun?" he taunted. "Come and take it."

Tulley's chest rose and fell. The banter was over and Darby knew the man was ready to stand and fight. Well and good.

The giant charged and Darby bobbed one way, then threw his weight behind a sizzling waist-high boomer that connected right over the belt buckle and made his foe jackknife in pain. Darby pivoted and lashed out while still off balance. His fist glanced off Tulley's ear, and he felt his legs being kicked out from under him.

He came down hard and rolled as Tulley hit the dirt impression he'd made with drawn knees. Both men scrambled erect.

This time, there was no hesitation. No feigning or weaving or bobbing. They came together like two rams, each going to take the other's head off his shoulders. Because of Tulley's reach, he connected first. Darby staggered and seemed to fall back. It was a ring-savvy trick he'd used many times to draw a taller man into him, into close fighting where his enormous arms could snap ribs and punish the heart until it was gone.

He ducked his head into Tulley's shoulder and started pounding. His fists traveled only inches but each one rocked his man a foot back. Darby knew he was being hit alongside his head, in his trunklike neck, on his shoulders. But they didn't hurt. And, for every one of Tulley's wild blows, Darby punched in two.

The giant was going back faster now, trying to open up some space and use his reach. Darby had no intention of letting that happen. Fists blurring, flesh pounding into flesh, great lungs going like bellows, he continued forward almost like Claude's dance partner.

The giant began to wince and backpeddle faster. In his haste, he tripped and spilled. Darby noted the familiar sight of fear starting to crawl into his opponent's eyes.

When the man was up, Darby attacked. Once again, he caught a boot in the thigh and it had power enough to half spin him around.

Tulley saw his opening and lunged. His huge fist swept in and snapped the writer's head back. Tulley's confidence soared and he closed exactly as Darby wished. The former pattern emerged and Darby sent every ounce of strength he had into his blows. His head was down and he knew a mean satisfaction in watching Tulley's feet lift off the ground with every punch.

The giant was finished, only he didn't know it yet. Darby let him step back; then he hammered a crunching fist into Tulley's jaw that sent him reeling off balance.

Darby never gave him a chance. He punched him from low and high—low to bend him over, then high to straighten him up.

When the man sobbed out for mercy and covered his battered face, Darby took a half step forward and drove an uppercut into the unprotected belly that lifted Tulley a foot off the dirt and dropped him like a fallen tree.

It was over. Darby watched the man go into a fetal position and squirm around in agony. He felt neither remorse nor pity. Had he wished, Darby could have finished Claude Tulley earlier but, instead, for Hank and Rollie and all those who'd died in the Paiute wars, he'd made the beating last. He'd stretched it out as far as he could, short of killing. Never, in all his fights, had Darby set out to physically abuse anyone so viciously. But none had deserved it until now.

Darby pivoted away in disgust. It would be a long and silent ride back to Carson City, and he intended to rope Tulley's hands behind his back. The man, though temporarily harmless, would recover soon and be as dangerous as ever.

Now, the thing to do was to find his horse and . . .

Darby jolted to a standstill. The blood in his legs jelled and a muscle began to twitch in his neck.

"Numaga!" he whispered.

The Paiutes sat motionless against the skyline and Darby had the feeling they'd been watching for a long time, waiting for the outcome as he and Tulley fought.

Darby swallowed drily. Numaga had given his warning, and he'd chosen to ignore it. The consequences seemed chillingly clear.

"Tulley," he whispered, "Get up! We've company."

The fallen man's transformation was nothing short of astounding. One glance at the waiting Indians and his eyes widened with fear while his complexion went as white as the salt flats.

He staggered to his feet, and they both saw an Indian begin pointing and gesturing wildly.

"My God," Tulley whispered. "That's him!"

"Who?"

"The girl's father. They must have . . ." his lips kept moving, but without sound.

"Have what? Tell me."

"That old Indian knows I was at Williams Station. That's why he's pointing at me. Look," he gasped. "He's fitting an arrow!"

Claude Tulley spied Darby's horse. "I'm going to get your rifle," he said, his voice rattling. "We're dead men, and they'll torture me first."

"Come back here."

"Go to hell," Tulley snapped as he staggered away.

Darby hurried over to find Tulley's Colt buried in the sage. It was loaded.

"Tulley!" he shouted. "There's been enough killing. I'm telling you to halt."

The giant faltered. Darby saw him glance up at the Paiutes. The father and what may have been his two sons all had their bows notched with arrows and were coming down the hillside.

Claude Tulley yanked Darby's rifle out and levered a bullet.

"Move," Darby roared, "and I'll kill you."

With his eyes still on the approaching Indians, Tulley shrugged. "You'd better, Mister, because my first bullet is for *you*."

Darby was no more than twenty feet from Tulley now. He could see a glaze over the man's eyes. Fear? Hatred? Resignation? Maybe all three.

Tulley pushed away from the horse. "If it hadn't been for you, I wouldn't be here," he mumbled brokenly.

"Drop the rifle." Darby raised his gun.

"Not a chance," Tulley said, raising the Winchester ever so deliberately.

"Blast," Darby swore in exasperation. He steadied his aim and reluctantly pulled the trigger. Down his gun sight, he could see Tulley buckle. Yet, the rifle was still in his hands and coming to rest against his thick shoulder.

Darby had no alternative. Tulley had said what he would do, and there wasn't any reason for bluffing now. So the writer fired twice more and was squeezing off a third shot when the big man began to fold.

There was a sharp barking order from the Indians and the three riders halted as Darby walked forward.

Claude Tulley was face down in the dirt, but Darby could hear the man's tortured breathing. He knelt down and rolled him over.

Stickers and gravel were plastered to his sweating face, and there was a film over his eyes that stared unseeing at eternity.

"Buckingham? Is that you?"

"Yes," Darby answered.

A crooked smile. "I outsmarted ya, Buckingham."

"Sure," Darby answered, not understanding or caring about the meaning of the words.

"I'm gettin' off easy. I . . . I heard they kill you slow. Too bad for you. And . . ."

"Is that why you didn't use that rifle any faster?" Darby asked softly.

Tulley coughed and blood bubbles frothed. "I'm . . . smart, ain't I? You don't get to see me hang and those . . . those redskins got cheated outa their fun. You . . ."

He shuddered, ground his teeth together, and his huge body convulsed. Darby bent forward and heard the man's dying words.

"You . . . lose."

Then, the last blood bubble popped and Tulley said no more.

Darby eased the man's head down and stood as the Indians let out a war whoop and came charging off the hillside.

There were two bullets left in his gun. Maybe he *should* get smart and use them on himself. Doesn't matter, he thought. Tulley was right—he'd lost.

Chapter 13

Darby was still unsure of what to do with those two bullets as the warring Paiutes swarmed down on him. If he was meant to die now, it would be far better to do so in battle than to take the coward's way out and shoot himself. Ironically, he thought about his readers those last few moments. What a black betrayal it would be to them if he took his own life.

Maybe Bolivar Roberts would find evidence that Darby had fought well his last gallant moments. If so, this information would eventually be transmitted back to his editor, J. Franklin Warner, in New York. His own notes on the Pony Express would be gathered and forwarded to New York. Probably some lesser but promising writer would be commissioned to put the manuscript together, and the story would be told after all.

Ahh, Darby thought, raising his gun and bracing himself for death, how I would have loved to write this, the final chapter of my own ending. Being taken from this world was a bitter thing, yet not being able to write about his own valiant, dying stand was nothing less than a tragic injustice.

Darby's pistol swung from Numaga, to the girl's father, to a nameless face. He had no wish to kill any of them, so he finally decided he would shoot the first Indian who fired.

Numaga's voice thundered over the hoof beats and, a hundred feet away, they slid to a gravel-rolling, dust-boiling standstill. For a moment, the world seemed to hang arrested. Then, Numaga alone prodded his mount forward.

"Throw down your gun, Darby Buckingham. You will ride with me now."

"Where?" he asked, dropping the weapon and feeling a surge of hope.

"To the place where my people stay. To where they grow weak and die."

Darby nodded and mounted his horse. Numaga hadn't *asked* him to go, he'd ordered him to do so and left no room for debate.

The Paiutes turned their horses and started away with Darby following. Yet, the three who'd first drawn their bows held back. Darby hesitated, and a warrior said something harsh enough to make him decide to do as he'd been told. But at the crest of the hill he reined in and looked down to the place they'd left.

Quickly, he looked away. The trio were leaping over the mutilated remains of big Claude Tulley. They began to chant and their voices carried up the hill and into the desert beyond. It was a haunting lament, a shrill primitive challenge, most likely passed down from a time when life was good. Darby hadn't any real knowledge of what they were chanting, but the grisly scene burned into his mind, and he knew he would remember it until the day that he died.

Perhaps a day like tomorrow.

They rode into the southern part of the Black Rock desert where Numaga and his people had been forced into hiding. It was a terrible wasteland, vast and arid; alkali plains stretched like a creeping disease about the feet of dark, volcanic mountains. He saw rugged craters and passes which could not be broached by cannons and military wagons.

Darby was appalled when he saw this country. It must have been very hard for Numaga to lead his old, his little children, the sick, and the women into such a land. Yet, the writer could tell that it was a sanctuary from his enemies. Every mile through those black rocks and canyons, he saw a hundred places where the chief might stage an ambush. Trails seemed to wander and circle and go nowhere, leading one deeper and deeper into a maze.

But what good was it all if this race of people died

from starvation? This he asked late at night as he was summoned to the Paiute council.

"Sit and be still, Darby Buckingham, and smoke the pipe in peace."

Darby nodded meekly. Besides the dominating form of Numaga, there were six others in the tent. The chief smoked first, then the long pipe traveled around the council circle and each man puffed without making a sound. Even before the pipe reached the writer, he knew he was in for a bad smoke. Whatever it was stunk like scorched pig fat. But he resolved that they would never know his feelings.

So he puffed, gagged, and puffed again before handing the pipe along. The tent became so foul and murky he thought he was going to pass out before it was over. Incredibly, the pipe stayed lit long enough to go around the council four more times.

"Now, we will talk."

Darby tried to fan the air enough to see Numaga across the circle. "Why have you spared me?" he gasped, breaking into a hacking cough.

Numaga glowered, then rose and opened the tent flap for air. There was an undeniable look of disgust as he resumed his place and waited for the smoke to clear.

"I have repaid my debt, and I was glad that you killed our enemy."

Darby leaned forward. Here was his opening. If he waited a moment too long, it would be gone. "Chief," he graveled, "and all you other gentlemen, I've proof about Williams Station. If it is your will, I shall go and seek a peace between our peoples. And . . ."

Numaga held up an outstretched hand. "One moment," he said. "I must interpret your words."

"Sorry." Darby waited as the Paiute Chief repeated in his own language. When he was finished, Darby opened his mouth to go on, but the council members erupted into an angry discussion.

"What's wrong?" Darby shouted over the voices.

The chief smashed the peace pipe down into the campfire ashes. Everyone lapsed into silence. Numaga glared around the council and his gaze finally rested on

Darby. "They say you lie. That there can be no peace.
They tell me you will only trick the Paiutes."

"And you?" Darby asked, his focus riveted on the
chief. "Is that what you think?"

Numaga's eyes drilled through him. "Your people
come and they take from my people. Our food, our
horses, our women."

Darby swallowed. He wasn't about to deny there'd
been wrongdoing; yet the Paiutes burning and looting
the Pony Express Stations wasn't right either. But, sur-
rounded by accusation, pressed tight among these Indian leaders, he knew better than to make the latter
point. He had to be diplomatic and, above all, not
promise the impossible or what he couldn't stand behind.

"Darby Buckingham, you must know that my people
want to return to our home, to live in peace and watch
our great lake change colors as the sun travels across
the sky, to fish and trap the birds as we have done
since the first days of time." His eyes were troubled.
Deeply so. "I have lost many young men. Their children will never study the ways of their fathers. My
people are sad and they are without spirit in this land.
We ask nothing but to be left alone. Is this so much,
Darby Buckingham?"

"No," he whispered. "It is not."

Numaga nodded. "Before many moons, the nights
will grow cold and the leaves will fall. At that time, my
people should gather cones from the pine nut tree and
prepare for the ritual of tasting the first good nut meat.
This they have always done."

His eyes shone. He seemed to stare deeply into the
past and his expression lost its harshness. "We dance
and sing for the fall harvest and ask our Father to protect the growing cones from sickness. And when the
ceremony is past, we hunt and prepare for the day
when our scouts bring news that the harvest is waiting
for our people. It was good, Darby Buckingham. In
those days, our women laughed, and our children were
not hungry and played games. In those days, my
people were happy."

"Chief," Darby said quietly. "Those days *can* return again."

"You say," he mumbled. "But what of your soldiers? Even now, they wait by our home. They have destroyed our karnees. We cannot go back!"

Darby pulled the written account of Hank Brown from the inside of his pocket and handed it across the fire. He pleaded with Numaga to let him present the document to Colonel Lander and make a bid for peace.

Numaga translated the paper out loud to the council and received quite a stir of agreement. The chief lifted his great hand and there was silence. He handed the paper back to Darby and gazed into the fire for a long, long time before he spoke.

"Those words are true. Did you write them?"

"Yes."

"Are you a writer?"

"Yes."

"Let me see your words in books."

Darby shook his head. "I . . . I don't have any with me. There are a few back in Carson City but . . ."

"Have you written of this trouble?"

"Well," he hedged, "I came out here to do a story on the Pony Express. And, of course, you and your warriors are part of it. But it isn't a book yet."

Numaga digested this very carefully. He asked a few more questions, then spoke to his council. There was an impassioned discussion this time. Darby awaited what he felt must be some kind of verdict. At this point, he had no idea what would happen.

Around the campfire, each man spoke his mind and the chief listened. It took them the better part of an hour but, when they were finished, the council was obviously in agreement.

"We have reached our mind," Numaga said decisively. Darby's heart began to beat faster. "A small party of my warriors will lead you from these black rocks. By night, you will travel into Carson City. You will find these . . . notes and give them to my warriors who will hide by the river. They will not wait long and you must not change your words."

"But they're not finished!"

Numaga ignored his outburst. "I will read them to my council. If they are true as the words we have already seen, I will talk peace with your Colonel Lander." His eyes flashed. "But, if they lie, we will fight until the death. Your Pony stations will fall and we will steal your horses for our battles."

Darby sighed with resignation. To predict how Numaga would react to his story was impossible. Yet, this was the thread of hope he'd asked for. The last thing he'd have wished was that peace would depend on his personal notes, notes in which he'd tried to tell both sides and, yet, they were dominated by his own commitment to the Pony Express. He just didn't know.

"When will I leave?"

"After you have eaten."

His belly rumbled with gratitude, but he ignored it. "How will I know your decision?"

Numaga almost smiled. "You will know, Darby Buckingham. The answer will sweep across our land as the eagle soars on desert winds."

Darby Buckingham, dirty, hungry, and heavily bearded, rode in and out of Carson City five days later sometime before sunrise. Though he still weighed considerably more than two hundred pounds, for a Buckingham, he would have been considered emaciated—a skeleton.

Not even Bolivar Roberts would have recognized his friend. His characteristic rolling gait was a bone-weary shamble, and his normally pink and healthy cheeks were a wind-and sunburnt mahogany.

In the few moments he was in his hotel room, he gazed with intense longing at his feather bed. And, though he denied himself its pleasure, he did light a Cuban cigar and shut his eyes in a kind of euphoria.

But he didn't stay more than a few minutes, only long enough to gather his notes. Would he ever see them again? Those immediate impressions would be gone forever. It would set him back weeks, and perhaps he'd never be able to rewrite his story with the freshness of life that it deserved.

It didn't matter. Not in comparison to the stakes

which were being played. So, with a resigned shake of his head, Darby gathered them together and slipped quietly out of the hotel and returned to the night.

An hour later, with the sunrise glowing to the east, he met the Paiutes and silently handed his writing away. The warriors said nothing, but they studied him well before reining their ponies and disappearing into the horizon.

Darby sat on his horse a long time and slowly puffed on his cigar until it was finished. A thousand questions burned in his mind. Over and over, he asked himself if he'd written a fair and unbiased account of this Pony Express War. And what had Numaga meant when he said the answer would sweep across the land as the eagle soars on desert winds?

He didn't know. Eagles were predators. They struck their victims quickly and without warning. The analogy did not bode well.

But it was done. He would shave and bathe and then eat and drink. Darby finally allowed himself to remember that steak he'd only sampled. It made him wheel his horse back toward Carson City, and he let it run. After the food, he would sleep—for days—and wait. Wait until the eagle soared.

It had been two weeks since the Pony Express entered Carson City. During that time, no mail had gone east or west, with the exception of that which he and Bolivar had carried with Lieutenant Perkins's protection.

Darby Buckingham was talking to Bolivar Roberts; small talk about nothing in particular. Then, from out in the street, they heard a cry.

"The Pony Express is acomin'!"

Both men jumped toward the street and raced around the corner in time to see the most beautiful sight imaginable—Pony Bob Haslam, standing up in his stirrups and waving his hat in triumph. They ran out to meet him along with half the people in Carson City.

"What happened? Is it clear? Did you see any Indians?" they all shouted at once.

Pony Bob dismounted and stretched. "Yeah," he drawled. "I saw Indians all right. In fact, I came face to face with the big chief himself."

"Numaga?" Darby whispered.

"Yep. I was out near Sand Springs when they boxed me in a canyon. Thought sure I was buzzard bait."

He hesitated, seeming to enjoy being the center of so much intense interest.

"Go on," Darby urged impatiently.

"Well, just as I was about to pull my gun, Numaga threw his war lance into the dirt and those Indians turned away. The chief was the only one who stayed. I was still a mite worried, 'cause he's a helluva big man. But you know what?"

"What?" Darby wished he would get on with his story.

"He rode up to give me a present."

Darby leaned forward, but Pony Bob wheeled away and opened a mail packet.

"He said for me to give you these papers, Mr. Buckingham."

Darby took his notes and his hands were trembling.

"Oh yeah, and there *was* one other thing."

"Well, tell me, damnit!"

The rider smiled. "He gave me this for you. Told me you'd understand."

Darby's throat swelled up and his chin quivered as he accepted the eagle feather. He understood now. Understood perfectly.

Darby had his notes and the end to his story. An ending far better than any he could have wished.

Truly, the eagle soared.

Epilogue

Though Darby Buckingham is a character of my imagination, most of the others in this story are not. Young Warren Upson and Pony Bob Haslam did make those historic rides as described, and the Pony Express was a courageous gamble by Messrs. Russell, Majors, and Waddell in hopes of acquiring the Central Overland Mail Route contract.

Bolivar Roberts, William Finney, and a remarkable cast made the impossible, possible. And, finally, I must say that the great Chief Numaga and the Paiute War played a dramatic role in the Pony Express story—a story far more sweeping and magnificent than can ever be adequately told.

In this page of history, the deeds transcend the legend.

INTRODUCING
GARY McCARTHY

Though I was raised in California, I grew up around horses and men who loved them. Men like Jonesey, one of the last of the old breed to actually participate in a Texas-to-Kansas trail drive. From fellas like that, I learned to ride and rope, to stick a bucking horse or barrel. In short, I wanted to be a cowboy.

So, I took a degree in Animal Science and then a higher one in Agricultural Economics. It was the second program that brought me to Nevada, where I spent a couple of years traveling the vast reaches of that state, meeting "real" cowboys. And, sometimes, during those years while I gathered the campfire stories, I saw lonely desert markers reminding me that I was in Pony Express country. Carson City was my home then, and right out in front of the State Museum there's a big memorial commemorating those riders. It seemed to me the Pony Express would never grow old in the telling and that my hero, the Derby Man, Darby Buckingham, ought to be the one who had the next whack at stirring it to life.

The Derby Man is no ordinary westerner. I like the fact that he's not just another tall, lean-hipped, fast-on-the-trigger shooter so common to most westerns. For even though he's not a crack shot and still insists on fine Eastern tailoring for his clothes, the Derby Man cuts a rock-hard heroic figure in the face of trouble. He also has the ability to laugh at himself when things go wrong. Darby Buckingham has grit. In coming stories, he's going to chronicle the West and, in spirit, I'll be with him all the way.

The Derby Man
The New Western Powerhouse

A Special Preview
of the exciting
opening pages of

SILVER SHOT

The new Derby Man adventure
by Gary McCarthy

Chapter 1

The heavy crunch of rolling ore wagons, the staccato popping of bullwhips, and the unending banter of drunken Virginia City miners filtered up from C Street but were ignored by the famous dime novelist. Darby Buckingham was deeply engrossed in putting down the final lines of his latest and best western novel, *The Pony Express War*.

As he penned the last sentences, Darby felt the rich sense of contentment and satisfaction that came to him only with the completion of a story well told. With a flourish, he wrote THE END and eased back in his chair. Wait, he thought happily, until his New York publisher, J. Franklin Warner, reads this one! Darby felt quite justified in allowing himself a rest and, for a few weeks at least, he would do nothing but lounge about, sip his favorite brandy, and enjoy that fresh shipment of Cuban cigars.

Yes, he needed time to increase his weight back to a respectable 255 pounds and rebuild his enormous strength up to the level of his circus strong man days. Darby flexed his right arm, tested its hardness. Not bad. From his desk drawer, he produced a tape measure and wrapped it around his mighty bicep. He was down only a quarter of an inch from his top form and was confident his personal weight-lifting program would soon negate the small loss.

Darby liked to eat, drink, and smoke his expensive cigars—and he even enjoyed testing his strength by hoisting whatever seemed challenging. But most of all, he liked to relax and think—think of his work and of Dolly Beavers, whom he would soon ask to come for a visit to help him wile away the hours with her exuberant charms. But not quite yet. Not until he had a chance to rest and regenerate his energies.

He was just about to pour himself a brandy and launch into reverie when he became aware that a violent quarrel was taking place in the street below.

"Conrad Trent! We know you're inside. Open the door and come out. We have to talk to you. It can't wait any longer."

Darby frowned, and tried to ignore the angry distraction that lifted upward.

"Look out, he's got a gun!"

"Hold it, driver! Move for that rifle and you're asking for trouble."

"I got him covered!"

"Mr. Trent. You owe us our mine back. We found it and it's ours!"

Darby Buckingham forgot about his drink and moved to the window. Everyone on the Comstock knew of Conrad Trent. Some said he was a saint and others thought he was the devil. In the few days that Darby had been in town, he'd heard the man's name whispered a dozen times and it never failed to create heated controversy. Now, Darby had the chance to see this Trent fellow and judge for himself the nature of the man. And, since he was in Virginia City to create another story, Conrad Trent might just have enough color to be useful.

"Mr. Trent, we don't want to come in after you, but so help me God we will. Open up!"

Darby brushed aside the curtains and poked his head out the window. In the middle of the street, he saw an ornate carriage, resplendent with silver fittings and gold handles, an impressive show of wealth made even more striking by a huge team of muscled sorrels whose coats shone like polished brass.

The source of the trouble was instantly apparent. A disreputable-looking fellow had grabbed the lead horse's bit and was struggling for control. His two young friends stood almost below Darby's window with poised rifles, angrily summoning Mr. Trent to disembark. All three appeared to be unwashed rabble, and Darby noticed they were very nervous, in contrast to the carriage driver who looked down upon the trio with contempt and, almost, anticipation. The driver had the lines in one hand but, in the other, a menacing blacksnake dangled into the street. He looked capable of using it at any moment.

The two riflemen seemed unsure. Both were young and either they had never felt the sun on their cheeks or else they were very scared, because their faces were white and bloodless.

"Mr. Trent. We just want our mine back." A long silence was broken by a cracked voice. "Mr. Trent, if you don't come out, we'll have to start shooting. We don't want it that way. Sir, you're leaving us precious little choice."

The silence grew taut as hundreds of onlookers waited with expectancy. One old man ventured a step out of the mob of onlookers. "Quinn Cassidy, you and your kid brother better turn and run while you've still got time. You're fixin' to get yourselves killed!"

There was a general murmur of agreement all around and the Cassidy brothers glanced worriedly at each other. Darby could almost smell their fear. Even from a distance of sixty feet, he could see how violently their rifle barrels quivered.

The lead horse was fighting for its head and starting to rear in its traces as the miner up front struggled to keep the animal under control. "Quinn," he called, "I can't hang onto this beast much longer!"

Quinn swallowed, then aimed his old muzzle-loader at the curtained window. "I'm going to count to five, Mr. Trent. Five is all, sir. Don't make me shoot."

The young man glanced around, saw the growing crowd of spectators and blinked the sweat of fear out of his eyes. "What are you all staring at!" he screamed.

No one answered. Most looked away.

"Why don't you go about your business instead of standing around gawking?" Still no answer. From Darby's vantage point he could tell that young Quinn Cassidy was very near breaking.

"Every one of you is afraid to speak out against the likes of Conrad Trent. But he didn't slick you outa a fortune like he did us. It ain't fair! All we're asking is to get our mine back. He ain't put one dollar of his own into our claim. It . . . it just ain't fair what he did and he ain't going to get away with it this time!"

Quinn cocked back the hammer and began to count. If he'd expected any sympathy or support, he now realized it wasn't coming. "One." A long pause. "Two."

Darby's sausage-thick fingers tightened down hard on the window frame when he saw the far-side carriage door begin to inch its way open.

"Three."

"Quinn Cassidy! You're making a big mistake."

The harsh warning bulled its way through the drawn curtains and muffled the count of four. "Listen carefully. I'm going to allow you exactly five minutes to get off the Comstock. If you aren't heading down this mountain by that time, I'll see you're buried proper in the morning."

Quinn's brother turned and Darby could see the wildness in the kid's eyes. He couldn't be more than thirteen and Darby watched him grab his older brother by the sleeve and whisper something urgent. Darby didn't have to read his lips to know the boy wanted to run.

"No," Quinn shouted harshly, "it's ours, not his! We've got to stand together, Patrick!"

Quinn straightened his thin and already work-stooped shoulders. On the off-side of the carriage, the door swung further outward.

"Listen to your kid brother and live to send wages back to Ireland," Conrad Trent ordered. "You've just four minutes left."

Darby leaned forward until his upper body was completely out the window. He couldn't explain it, but he had a dead certain feeling that the three young Irish miners were going to die.

The fools! It was like watching a tragedy unfold from the balcony seats of a theater. He wanted to shout a warning that a man was sneaking out of the carriage door. Maybe the fellow holding the team was supposed to guard against this very maneuver, but now all of his energies were concentrated on the fractious horse.

Darby saw a hat brim slide along the rooftop and knew what was going to happen.

"Quinn Cassidy," the voice from behind the curtains, purred, "I want you to listen very carefully to what . . ."

Darby whirled and raced to his closet. He threw open the door and groped inside until his fingers closed on his ever-faithful double barreled shotgun. Why was he getting involved in this trouble! Hadn't he just gotten out of enough dangerous situations while working on *The Pony Express War*? Virginia City was a violent town and with every day that passed at least one man was shot to death in some kind of quarrel.

He hesitated at the closet door. "Stay out of it, Buckingham," he growled.

The voice, so cool and reassuring, drifted in through his window. "Quinn," it soothed, "you're a good lad and you just had some bad luck. Run fast while there's still a chance for you and Patrick and Dave to live."

The voice. It was almost hypnotic: Resonant, reasonable, and yet—somehow deadly. The writer yanked his shotgun up and checked to make certain it was loaded. He wasn't going to use it, of course. This was none of his affair. Maybe the young trio's claims were totally unfounded. That was entirely possible. Or perhaps they'd been foolish enough to gamble away their new discovery and had decided to take it back at the point of a gun.

Darby snapped the breech of the shotgun closed and pivoted towards the window. He wasn't sure what he could do but at least he had to try and stop a senseless killing. Maybe he could cover everyone from his window until a peaceful solution could be found. Maybe . . .

"Quinn, look out!"

It was Patrick's voice. High and shrill like a terrified child. The warning was instantly pierced by gunfire.

Darby lunged for the window and yanked his rifle up, taking off a hunk of paint and wood.

The Cassidy brothers were on the ground and either dead or wounded while the one who'd been responsible for containing the horses was fleeing down the street. Everyone watched Conrad Trent, resplendent in a perfectly tailored white suit, flick his gun out of its holster.

"Right foot, through the heel!" he called to his staring audience. Then, without even appearing to bother
aiming, he fired. Darby's head snapped around and he
saw the runner cry and break stride as he pitched
headlong into the street and rolled in the dust grap-
pling for his right boot.

The carriage driver slapped his Winchester against
his shoulder and took aim at the fallen runner.

Overhead, Darby Buckingham also took aim but at
a different target.

"No!" Conrad Trent commanded. "Let him live.
Roan, I'm ordering you not to fire."

Darby gratefully eased the killing pressure off his
trigger, knowing full well that, from this distance, he'd
have peppered the street and maybe hit innocent
bystanders. Roan obeyed, but argued vehemently—
first, to kill, then just to horsewhip them until this day's
lesson was written on their backsides.

"He's dead!" Patrick wailed, seeming to regain con-
sciousness with a rush. "Quinn is dead!"

"It's his fault," Trent said dispassionately. He was a
big man, tall, solid, and ruggedly handsome with dark,
piercing eyes that seemed to go through the frail,
ragged boy at his feet. "If you were a man you'd be
dead as well. I don't shoot kids, even though you'd
have killed me."

He scanned the silent crowd, then reached into his
pockets and threw some money down at Patrick Cassidy. "That's for the decent burial I promised. After
Dave sees the doctor, you both are leaving the Comstock."

Patrick spat on the money, then he spat on the perfectly creased pantleg of Conrad Trent.

Trent's face flamed. He reached down, pulled the
boy to his feet, then drew back his fist and knocked
him spinning into the dirt.

Someone in the crowd swore and Darby Buckingham cursed so vehemently that Trent looked up at
him. Their eyes locked for an instant before the man
turned back and addressed what had now become a
clearly antagonistic group of witnesses.

"They would have killed me and I had every right to defend my good name. Is there any one of you who would not stand up to defend his own hard-earned reputation? A reputation of trust and confidence."

He lifted his arms dramatically. "Gentlemen, within your midst are plenty whom I have assisted to become prosperous. Yes, prosperous!"

"Not all of us, that's for damn sure!" an apron-wearing saloon keeper griped.

Darby saw a quick flick of anger rise on Conrad Trent's cheeks as he whirled to confront his detractor.

"Who said that!"

The speaker appeared to melt in stature and refused to identify himself.

Trent's face muscles relaxed and he laughed outright. "I know it was you, Jess Arnold. Come on, stand up tall and let those around you benefit from your mistakes."

Someone pushed Arnold to the fore and other men snickered at his quaking knees.

Trent did not seem to notice, but now appeared to be enjoying himself. "Jess, is it not true, when I doubled your stock, I then strongly advised you to sell at a profit? And did I not also demonstrate my conviction by divesting myself of that very same stock?"

Arnold's head bounced up and down like a cork on a fishing line. He wouldn't even meet Trent's eyes. Darby grunted with disgust. What a spineless excuse for a man!

Conrad Trent radiated righteous vindication. "There you have it. One more pitiable accusation set straight." His eyes scolded them all, then he smiled. "Gentlemen, I have, by my own reliable sources, just received some very valuable information relating to the stock market. And now I am about to take action based upon that information, and place several orders by telegraph to the San Francisco Stock Board. As a demonstration of my integrity, I am going to invite . . ."

Darby failed to catch the rest of the words. All eyes were on Conrad Trent like an actor on center stage. But Darby witnessed something else. He saw young

Patrick Cassidy's thin fingers inching towards his rifle—very, very slowly.

Darby choked back a warning as the thought struck him that Conrad Trent might very well use the time advantage as an excuse to kill the young Irishman. The writer pivoted and raced for his door. There was only one way to prevent another brutal killing and that was to reach Patrick before he could get his hands on that rifle. Darby barreled down the plushly carpeted hallway of Virginia City's finest hotel and leapt to the stairway, taking the steps three at a bound. He detested moving quickly; his short, thick legs were built for power, not speed. Yet, as he rushed down into the lobby, the image of those fingers spidering toward the rifle propelled him on. He would snatch the weapon out of reach before the young fool created the opportunity for his own demise. Then, then, by God he'd have a word or two for Mr. Conrad Trent! The man had obviously convinced the others that he'd reacted purely out of self-defense, but Darby disagreed. The trio seemed to be no more than scared kids begging for a hearing.

One thing was clear as Darby stormed across the lobby—if he was any judge of character at all, then the high and mighty Mr. Trent was an egocentric, spellbinding rattlesnake. In booting the defenseless Patrick, he'd earned Darby's lasting contempt.

The loud crack of rifle fire told Darby he was too late. Yet, even as he slammed through the doorway, he heard another sound. Not gunfire, but a sharp, popping noise. Darby collided with a spectator and knocked the man sideways as they both flew headlong into the street.

When he looked up, he realized the carriage driver called Roan was going to demonstrate the fine art of using a bullwhip. Darby saw Conrad Trent stoop to retrieve his ivory stetson from the dust, then poke a finger through a bullet hole in the brim. For a moment, everything seemed to hang suspended as the crowd's eyes were glued on the stockbroker. Then Conrad Trent ran his manicured fingers through his thick shock of silver-dusted hair and his chin dipped. Once.

That was all the signal Roan needed. The whip slashed across twenty feet of ground and bit the flesh out of Patrick Cassidy. It was so savage that Darby blinked before he roared with anger as his own voice joined Patrick's cry.

He'd left his shotgun upstairs realizing it would only result in more death, and he was unwilling to let himself be drawn into a crossfire between Conrad Trent, his driver, and the man who'd slipped out of the carriage unnoticed. Now, as he hurtled forward, he wished he'd brought the shotgun. Even before he'd traveled six feet, Roan had already snapped the whip again and was about to do so once more.

The quickness of arm and wrist drove the whip with unbelievable speed. It appeared to be at least twenty feet long, braided leather with a thick wooden handle.

"Stop!" Darby bellowed, trying to prevent even more damage.

Roan's eyes widened as he saw the big man coming in at a labored run. He probably had four seconds before Darby's outstretched hands could reach his throat—he needed less than two. Roan's weight pivoted on line and the whip retreated behind, then his wrist and arm pumped forward and the blacksnake's metal-tipped fang came toward Darby Buckingham.

Instinctively the dime novelist threw up a forearm to protect his eyes. The whip snaked across his lower legs and brought him crashing to the dirt. Even before he could recover, he heard the blacksnake whisper again and retreat.

"You'd better go for my throat," Darby rasped, "because I'm going for yours!"

"Come on, then!" Roan challenged. "Get up, big man, and I'll teach you how to mind your own business. Git!"

Darby was half erect, crouched and gathering himself to spring, when the whip flicked out and drove at his face. He twisted and tried to block its path but the metal tip slid by his arm and bit him over the ear.

He grabbed for it—but missed and wanted to shout with frustration.

"Come on!" Roan goaded, almost dancing with eagerness and blood-lust.

Darby charged with his arms up as protection. He heard Roan's laughter, then saw him maneuver sideways, shaking out the blacksnake just the way he wanted before throwing it to bite. The snake came in low again, intent on wrapping itself around his legs and tripping him down once more.

He bent and made a grab for the whip and was instantly sorry for the mistake. It was like gripping a fiery stick and it paralyzed his left hand.

Darby's breath was coming faster and he knew he was in no shape for this. Each time he charged he was slower, while Roan was barely exerting himself. It would only get worse unless he somehow changed the tide. As it was now, he had the feeling that Roan was just waiting for him to drop his hands and grab for the whip—that's when it *would* go for his throat.

Lying in the dust, feeling warm blood trickle down from the wound over his ear, hearing the crowd shout with excitement, and watching Roan make the whip behind him move like an expectant sidewinder, Darby had an idea. Not a brilliant one, but a desperate one. He had to maneuver Roan up against something so the man couldn't draw back the whip and send it forward.

Roan was standing ten paces in front of the lead carriage horse. Darby climbed to his feet and began to position himself for what he frantically hoped was his last charge.

"Come on, Mister. Quit trying to circle in on me!"

Darby's lips curled and he continued around just out of range. Now, he had the man's back to the horses. If he could just get close enough to make Roan retreat a few steps. Maybe the whip would get fouled under the horses' feet, maybe . . .

Maybe he was a fool. Roan was too clever to allow himself to be backed up close to an entanglement—twenty years of practice too clever.

Darby saw the man glance over his shoulder then begin to sidestep his way clear. There was nothing left now but to charge.

He threw his right forearm up before his face and

kept his other bloodied hand low and outstretched. The blacksnake came flying in at his knees. Fast. Nothing more than a blur and a hum. It struck and wrapped as Darby threw his legs apart and grabbed for leather. His hand was wet and, for a moment, he thought the whip was going to slip free to strike again.

But it didn't. It slid across his palm until the metal tip caught on his ring and then Darby's hand closed down tightly. He wanted to laugh when he saw Roan's face. Gone was the man's sneer and now he struggled despertely to pull free.

Darby made a quick circular motion, wrapping the leather around both hands, and then he gave the whip a brutal yank. The result was like snapping a carp out of its pond. Roan completely left the ground and hurled forward with his arms extended and still gripping his whip's handle.

When he flopped to earth, Darby pounced on him. He reached down and dug his fingers into the man's throat and, like an enraged bear, began to shake Roan senseless. Only an iron will and his last pain-filled bit of reason kept the ex-circus strong man from collapsing his victim's windpipe.

Only that—and the gun barrel that cracked against his skull.

The Derby Man is down but don't count him out as he confronts treachery and danger in the midst of an explosive silver boom town.

Read the complete Derby Man adventure, SILVER SHOT, available soon wherever Bantam Books are sold.